*This book is set in Victorian England
when attitudes and language differed from those of today.
As a result certain phrases used and attitudes
depicted might cause offence.*

Just Wheatley?

Barry Silsby

Just Wheatley?

Vanguard Press

VANGUARD PAPERBACK

© Copyright 2023
Barry Silsby

A CIP catalogue record for this title is
available from the British Library.

ISBN 978 1 80016 764 3

*Vanguard Press is an imprint of
Pegasus Elliot Mackenzie Publishers Ltd.*
www.pegasuspublishers.com

First Published in 2023

**Vanguard Press
Sheraton House Castle Park
Cambridge England**

Printed & Bound in Great Britain

The thin metal shaft glistens with blood. I drop it to the pebbles, hear the chink of it landing, take a glance at the body, look away. So still. Dead? Was it me? I remember the taunting, the anger, the refusal to see reason. But most of all the taunting. Needing to make it stop. But not the blood. Where has the blood come from? Think!

I disguise the damage as best I can, remove the evidence, crunch away through the shingle. They'll think it's a drowning washed up here under the pier. They will, won't they?

If only I could remember. I don't remember the blood. But I do know one thing. Only one. It was deserved. Wasn't it? I'm sure it was deserved...

Friday 2nd February 1894

If you enter Brighton Police station via the double doors under the blue lantern kept permanently burning, you enter from Bartholomews on street level. However, if you continue past the front desk — though this is unlikely as it is always staffed by Sergeant Johnson who will certainly send you on your way with a flea in your ear unless you have a cast-iron reason for being there, and even if you do he is likely to keep you waiting for as long as he feasibly can — but if you *were* to proceed across the parading hall and past the cubby-hole laughingly known as the Detective Office, you would rapidly realise that you are now below ground. The magnificent edifice of Brighton Town Hall was constructed on the side of a hill and most of the police station built into the side of it. Past the Detective Office is a narrow staircase. Down these stairs are two more basement levels, the first housing the cells and the police constables' locker room with ablutions and storerooms below that, damp, dark, dingy places to be sure. But climb those same stairs and suddenly you are aware of opulence and sunlight. This level is usually entered via the columned and porticoed main entrance. It is the setting for the magistrate's court and it is on this floor that the Chief

Constable and the Inspector of Detectives have their offices.

As he reached the top of the narrow staircase, Detective Wheatley paused to wonder at the contrast between the utilitarian police station he had just left and the grandeur of the Town Hall proper. Here, marble rather than concrete was underfoot and he strode across the Brighton Coat-of-Arms inlaid into the floor, past mahogany-panelled corridors to knock on the door marked *J. A. Cronin Esq., Inspector of Detectives*. Hearing the word 'Come' in answer to his knock, Wheatley entered the office, closing the door carefully behind him. The room was large and high-ceilinged with a mahogany desk set before a substantial window looking across the Market Square and down towards the sea. An expensive-looking Turkey carpet occupied the space in front of the desk while opposite was a fireplace surrounded by sparsely inhabited bookshelves. Adjacent to the fireplace stood two green leather buttoned chairs. The Inspector was sitting in one of these before a roaring fire, his face buried in the *Brighton Gazette and Sussex Telegraph*.

Wheatley wondered whether he was supposed to sit in the other chair but decided to assume an 'at ease' pose until invited to do so. It was a cold, January day but even so the room was exceedingly hot and Wheatley remembered that on his last foray into the inspector's office a similar fire had been burning despite the mild day. *Perhaps the Inspector feels the cold*, he thought to himself before saying out loud, "You sent for me, sir?"

"Ah, Edwards," came from behind the newspaper.

"Wheatley, sir," interrupted Wheatley.

This caused the newspaper to be lowered slightly so that the inspector could peer over it at the young detective. "I thought I sent for Edwards," he said.

"PC Jupp said that I was to come if Edwards was unavailable," Wheatley replied. "I hope that is correct sir."

"Yes, quite so. Edwards unavailable, eh? Where is he then?"

"Out pursuing enquiries, sir," Wheatley replied, supplying the usual excuse for when Detective Edwards did one of his many disappearing acts and hoping fervently that the inspector would not enquire about the enquiries.

He didn't.

"Oh well, you'll have to do," he said, dropping the newspaper to the floor. Wheatley eyed the newspaper nervously, thinking it far too close to the flames in the grate for comfort.

"And what is that you've got there?"

Wheatley looked down and realised that in his haste he was still holding the silver-topped Malacca cane that he had been idly polishing when summoned.

"Part of a raid on a fence in Church Street this morning, sir. Probably stolen property."

"Well, put it down, man, you look nervous enough without constantly fiddling with that." Adding, "On the desk, detective," as he noticed Wheatley looking around confusedly for some place to put it.

Wheatley walked across and placed the cane carefully onto the shining desktop, which contained only a foolscap-sized blotter, a perpetual calendar and an ornate pen and ink stand. Wheatley couldn't help noticing the leather-bound blotter was pristine. Nothing had been blotted on it for a while. He returned to stand in front of the inspector.

"Nice stick, that," said the inspector. "Stolen, did you say?"

"Suspected so, sir, though it doesn't match anything on the 'reported stolen' list."

"Really?" The inspector closed his eyes as if in thought for a moment, then asked, "Now, what did you want?"

"Err, you sent for me, sir."

"Did I? Ah, so I did. Sir Toby."

"Sir?" said Wheatley.

"Do keep up, Wheatley," said the inspector, taking a folded piece of paper from his inside jacket pocket and handing it to the detective together with a visiting card which read 'Sir Tobias Hughes-Lewthwaite, baronet,' on the front and had a London address on the obverse.

"He's an acquaintance of mine, came to Brighton for the season, took a house on the Steyne, then stayed because of his niece's poor health." The inspector paused and looked expectantly at Wheatley.

"Poor health, sir?" said Wheatley, at a loss as to what he was expected to do with the proffered information.

"Not poor health, that's neither here nor there, what has the girl's poor health got to do with her disappearance?"

"Disappearance, sir?"

"Are you being deliberately obtuse? The girl has disappeared. That is why you're here. To find her. It's all on the piece of paper I gave you."

And when Wheatley looked, there was indeed a full report. Age and description of the missing girl, what she had last been seen wearing. When she had last been seen. And the address on the Steyne where she and her uncle had been staying. *Not the best address*, thought Wheatley, *too far north for that*. In fact, hardly on the Steyne at all. Not one of those with a view of the late king's wonderful Oriental Palace. Nor those with a view of the gardens and down to the sea. But a presentable address all the same.

"I told him I'd put my best man on it," said the inspector.

"But you'll have to do," he added. Wheatley looked up from the report to see Inspector Cronin scrabbling for his newspaper, obviously thinking the interview was over. Wheatley cleared his throat and held his ground.

"Yes, what is it?" asked the inspector.

"Well, sir, I was wondering if we should expect foul play?"

"I shouldn't think so. Silly girl wandered off, or got involved with some gigolo. You know the type, I expect. Probably home snivelling her eyes out by now."

Wheatley wasn't sure he did know the type but decided to pursue other avenues of enquiry.

"Any thought that the uncle might be involved in her disappearance?"

"Certainly not, the fellow is of the best sort. A fellow traveller, if you get my drift."

"Traveller, sir?" said Wheatley.

"Of course, Wheatley, he's on the level, capital chap."

Wheatley was now completely confused, but the inspector was in no mood for further questioning.

"That will be all, Wheatley," he said, returning to his newspaper.

"Just a couple of que—"

"That will be all, Detective," said the inspector forcefully and returned to his newspaper muttering the words 'needs spoon feeding,' clearly heard by Wheatley as he left the room. Closing the door behind him, Wheatley realised that he had left the Malacca cane on the inspector's desk. Briefly, he considered returning for it but deciding on discretion he turned back to the stairs and descended to the depths of the Detective Office.

*

Detective Wheatley had obtained the Malacca cane just that morning from Jakub Zimmerman, businessman, pawnbroker and suspected fence. Wheatley, the youngest and newest recruit to the Brighton Municipal Constabulary's Detective Office had stood beneath the sign of the three golden balls looking in through the glass door of the pawn shop, on the corner of Church Street and Jew Street, 'Jakub Zimmerman, Pawnbroker and Purveyor of Fine Goods' sign written on the glass. The window to his right contained a cacophony of poor items, pledged but never redeemed. Threadbare coats and battered hats shared space with dented cooking pots and chipped crockery. To protect these treasures, the glass in the window was covered by a stout metal grid, as was the door in front of him. The door was locked and Wheatley leaned forwards to peer into the dim interior of the shop. Dividing the space was a counter behind which sat a man of some age peering out at the detective. Another stout grid filled the space from the countertop to the ceiling while an iron-barred door gave access to the rest of the shop and the storeroom beyond. Behind the counter, shelves and cubby holes were filled with small items awaiting redemption while a rack of clothes of all sorts stood against the side wall of the shop along with various trunks, stands and packing cases.

The man behind the counter continued to stare at Wheatley, then, seeming to make up his mind that here was a genuine customer, adjusted his shawl with a shrug and moved his hand under the counter. There was a buzz and the door released. Wheatley entered the premises and heard the snick of the door locking itself after him, noting the modern and very expensive security system that seemed so at odds with the contents of the shop.

"*Shalom*. Am I addressing Mr Zimmerman?" said Wheatley. The man behind the counter maintained his silence. Now that he could see him clearly, Wheatley realised that the man was even older than he had originally appeared. His skin was heavily wrinkled, his sidelocks and beard grey and straggling. Despite wearing an ancient fedora and a heavy overcoat and wrapped tightly in his *tallit*, the man appeared cold, slumped on his high stool behind the counter. Wheatley realised he had been staring for some time and hastily looked away, sweeping the room for an excuse for his presence.

"I've come to look for…" Wheatley wondered what he *had* come to look for. Or what he could say he had come to look for. In reality he was looking for stolen property but he couldn't say that, this being a reconnaissance mission and him incognito.

"I need a… a walking stick," he said as his eyes lit on an umbrella stand containing a jumble of sticks and umbrellas next to the rack of old clothes on the shop floor. He looked back to the old man. He continued staring. Then, just as Wheatley was wondering if the old man was deaf or simple, he removed his right hand from beneath his shawl and agonisingly slowly indicated the umbrella stand before returning his hand to the snug warmth of his armpit.

Taking this for permission, Wheatley crossed the shop to examine the contents of the rack. As he expected, there were umbrellas with tines bursting from their fabric, others without handles. In between was a motley collection of sticks, some serviceable bentwood types while others appeared to be ripped straight from the tree. A sad collection all told and Wheatley was about to give up when he noticed a metallic glint from within the folds of a particularly sorry-looking umbrella. Disentangling the fabric, Wheatley pulled out a fine-looking cane. The stick was scuffed and dull but could be Malacca, and the finial, though tarnished, might well be silver. Wheatley wet his finger and scrubbed at the collar of the cane. He swore he could see the lion *passant* stamped into it. A thorough polish and it would be a fine cane indeed.

"I rather like this one," he said, taking it to the counter.

The old man stretched his hand between the bars of the counter and drew the cane through them, holding it between his hands and staring at it.

"Ah, such a stick," he said. "You have a good eye, young gentleman. What a stick, indeed."

Wheatley waited. When he could stand the silence no longer, he said, "I assume it's for sale."

The old man looked down at the cane for a few more seconds, then placed it gently on the countertop, rested his hands on either side of it and looked up into Wheatley's face.

"Is ever such a stick really for sale? Can we say that such a stick is ever truly owned?" The old man nodded at his own wisdom, sighed, then said, "I suppose I could let it go."

Wheatley waited. The old man was looking down at the cane again, nodding. Then he raised his eyes and said, "Such a stick. Such a stick will cost you two guineas."

Wheatley gasped aloud at the sum asked, almost twice his weekly wage. "Two guineas?" he stuttered, quite forgetting that his 'purchase' was all pretence.

"Well, I could possibly go to two pounds." A beat of silence, then, "And one shilling."

Wheatley was just about to say that it was too rich for him and leave, when he realised how distracted he'd become from the main purpose of his visit. He stood as if contemplating the price and stared over the old man's shoulder at the items displayed on the shelves and in the cubby holes behind him. The more he looked the more he recognised items similar to those on the 'reported stolen' list he had memorised before setting off on a tour of pawnshops that morning. That silver snuffbox there could possibly be one reported stolen from a house on the Steyne. Other items looked familiar but he must have been staring too hard, for suddenly the old man's head whipped round and the cane disappeared beneath the counter.

"What are you gawking at?"

"Nothing," said Wheatley hastily, "just trying to work out how I could pay for it. Would you take one pound ten shillings?" A plan was forming in Wheatley's mind. With the start of bargaining, the old man seemed placated and the cane reappeared on the counter.

"Are you trying to bankrupt me, young man?"

Eventually they settled on one pound, seventeen shillings and ninepence. Wheatley had told the old man that he would return with the money that afternoon as he didn't have such a large sum about his person. The proprietor seemed satisfied with that, turning to place the stick on a shelf behind him before operating the door release, allowing the young detective to leave. Wheatley returned to the police station and spent the rest of the day organising a raid on the shop.

*

"Is this where all the Jew-boys live then?"

Detective Edwards, officially Wheatley's mentor but in fact the other half of the strength of the detective office, stood at the end of the twitten that led from Jew Street to the parallel Bond Street and gazed up at the road sign attached to the brickwork above his head.

Wheatley, his eyes fixed at the end of the road where shop lay, paused before answering. He wondered that he still felt a surge of anger whenever talk was so disparaging about his mother's people. His people, too, he supposed. But he had learned very early in his working life that employers, and particularly the police, were not disposed to sympathetic treatment of those they still considered 'Christ Killers' and he had learned to hide his heritage, subsuming any hurt he felt.

"Several Hassidic families do live in this area," he replied eventually, "But the name really originates with Brighton's first synagogue which was built here in towards the end of the last century."

"Where's that then?" asked Edwards, blowing on his hands and rubbing them together before pushing them once more, deep into the pockets of his overcoat. "All I can see around here are slums, knocking shops and shyster warrens." Edwards was not pleased at being called out on active duty on a frosty winter's day and certainly not to this insalubrious area.

"Wasn't here long, moved after ten years or so," said Wheatley. He gazed around at his surroundings. The area was certainly run-down but the remnants of one or two fine houses could be seen beneath the dirt and soot and general neglect amongst the ramshackle workshops and tenements.

"How do you know these things, Wheatley?" mused Edwards. Then, shivering dramatically, he turned down the twitten, calling, "Shan't be long, brass monkey's here," over his shoulder as he went.

"Shouldn't we wait?" Wheatley called. "Surely the sergeant can't be much longer?" But seeing it was useless, his words bouncing off the detective's disappearing back, returned to his scrutiny of the street's end.

Minutes ticked by. Many minutes. Alone, Wheatley found his mind wandering. How *did* he know these things? Well, most things he picked up easily, was always surprised when others didn't. But this street, this street of course, was in his memory for personal reasons.

"Wheatley, I. M., M. I. Wheatley." He spoke aloud, then looked about him to check no one was around to hear. He had been born to loving parents who constantly argued, usually about religion. His mother came from a Jewish family, disowned when she ran away to marry Wheatley's

20

father. A gentile. A Christian, that was bad enough, but even worse, a Catholic. Their arguments came to a head when Wheatley was born. After the joy and tears of the birth came the tribulation and tears of the registration. Wheatley had never seen his birth certificate but he had heard the story enough times from one disgruntled parent or another to know that the battles that raged throughout his childhood began there. It hardly affected him until his schooling began, a schooling that would be disrupted throughout its entire eight years. When his mother was in the ascendancy, he would be sent to Schule at the synagogue in Devonshire Place as Isaac M. Wheatley. When his father reasserted his authority, he would be transferred to St Joseph's School for Catholic boys as Matthew I. Wheatley. Wheatley smiled as he remembered his parents, always vexed about religion, always arguing about anything that came into their heads, sniping at one another between the heavy silences. And always completely and utterly in love. They had died within a week of each other, one from influenza, the other from grief. Literally a broken heart.

However, constantly changing schools and cultures had never been easy and even now he was unsure whether he was Wheatley M.I. or Wheatley I.M. and used his initials interchangeably whenever he had to complete official forms. To his few acquaintances and colleagues he answered to Wheatley, and in the unlikely event of anyone asking him for his first name he always answered, "Call me Wheatley; just Wheatley."

Lost in his reverie, he suddenly became aware of movement behind him and turned to come face to face with Sergeant Johnson and two hefty constables. Not, of course, literally face to face. All three uniformed policemen were a good head taller than Wheatley and at least twice as wide.

"Well," said Sergeant Johnson, pausing to clear his throat and spit a spume of phlegm stained brown with tobacco juice into the central gutter, "can't stand here dilly-dallying waiting for you, detective. Let's get on," before turning on his heel and striding off.

The two constables followed, leaving Wheatley floundering. He knew he should be saying that he had been at the rendezvous on time, that it was Sergeant Johnson who had kept *him* waiting, that... But he knew no good would come of his words even if he found the courage to confront the sergeant. So, swallowing his ire and with a glance down the ominously empty twitten in the hope that Detective Edwards was returning, he hurried to catch up with the three policemen before they spooked the old man and ruined the whole operation.

He caught up with them just before they reached the end of Jew Street, stopping before a door which was possibly a side entrance to the pawn shop. Leaving them concealed around the corner, Wheatley stepped into Church Street and presented himself at the shop door. No response from inside. Stooping to peer through the barred glass he could see the same old man huddled behind the counter as if he had not moved since that morning. The man was staring directly at Wheatley, who tried waving, then in a moment of inspiration removed a half-crown from his waistcoat pocket and held it up so it was clearly visible. Instantly there was a buzz from the door and Wheatley was able to enter. As he stepped over the threshold, Wheatley stood with his back to the door, holding it open and was relieved to see Sergeant Johnson and the two constables piling forwards. At the appearance of the police uniforms, the shopkeeper's hand moved, rapidly this time, beneath the counter. Wheatley distinctly heard three groups of three rings echoing from the rear storeroom before Sergeant Johnson was rattling the bars of the door next to the counter, screaming, "Get this fucking door open you whoreson of a kike," while the shopkeeper made great show of trying one wrong key after another in the lock.

Wheatley left them to it, exiting the shop and moving swiftly to the street corner. He arrived in time to see a young man exit from the door onto Jew Street and saunter towards the nearby twitten, a full sack over his shoulder. As the man approached the twitten, Wheatley was relieved to see the substantial figure of Detective Edwards appear from it. Nonchalantly tapping a solid police truncheon into his left hand, he stepped into the man's path. The young man turned, only to see Wheatley blocking the other end of the street. Reacting quickly, the man threw his sack at Edwards, then turned and ran back the way he had come, presumably deciding to take his chance on overpowering the much slighter, and unarmed, Wheatley. Wheatley clenched his fists, but even he doubted that this would discourage the young man who had pulled a knife from somewhere about his person and was barrelling towards the detective. Wheatley faced his inevitable demise, steeling himself to do his duty and desperately trying to banish the images of himself lying bleeding onto the icy ground, when suddenly the side door from the pawnbroker's slammed back and Sergeant Johnson emerged. The man with the knife skidded to a halt, now faced by two opponents with a third panting up behind. Sergeant Johnson, though, needed no help. His stick crashed down on the man's knife-hand, then backhanded across his throat felling him. Johnson followed up with several kicks of his size ten boots into the man's body for good measure.

"Sergeant Johnson, stop!" shouted Wheatley, who wanted his man in the cells, not in the Sussex County Hospital, nor, as looked more likely with the sergeant in a real temper, the mortuary.

Surprisingly, the sergeant did stop. Panting heavily, he said, "Fair enough, Wheatley, your collar. Your collar." Then with a final kick to the man's kidneys, Sergeant Johnson turned back through the door into the pawn shop.

That kick ensured that the young man was ready to go quietly when arrested. While Wheatley and Edwards picked up the loot, the pawnshop proprietor and his young accomplice, both handcuffed, were marched off to the police cells under the Town Hall by the two uniformed constables. As expected, most of the items collected had been reported as stolen and Detective Edwards had gone for a celebratory pint at the Star and Garter Hotel, leaving Wheatley to complete the inventory of the fenced goods.

Wheatley had picked up the cane which had first attracted his attention earlier that morning and was just about to get to work on the silver top when there was a knock and P.C. Jupp's head had appeared around the door.

"Inspector wants to see Detective Johnson," he said, looking around as if wondering if Johnson was hiding somewhere in the tiny office. "Or you," he added. "If Johnson's not here." With that, the constable closed the door, only to open it again to say, "By the way, good result today, Mr Wheatley. Well done." The door was almost closed again when he added, "I'd get up to see the inspector pretty rapidly if I was you, lad."

And now the Malacca cane was in the office of the Inspector of Detectives, and was likely to remain there until Wheatley had solved the case of the missing young lady.

Monday 5th February 1894

"Tradesman's entrance in the basement."

Wheatley's knock on the door of number 28, Grand Parade, had been answered by a footman who attempted to slam the door in the face of the young policeman. Wheatley was a relatively new detective but he had done his apprenticeship as a patrolman in the Brunswick Town Watch and still wore the stout, highly polished boots of a police constable. The footman's attempt at slamming the door rebounded back from one of the said boots, which Wheatley had inserted next to the door-jamb. Such was the force of the rebound that the footman had to jump back to avoid injury. Taking advantage of this, Wheatley stepped over the threshold, removed his hat and held it out towards the startled servant.

"Detective Wheatley, Brighton Municipal Constabulary, to see Sir Tobias Hughes-Lewthwaite."

Recovering quickly, the footman resumed his haughty manner, staring first at the bowler hat, then at Wheatley, then back to the hat again but making no attempt to take it.

"You do realise that it is an offence to obstruct a police officer in the performance of his duty?" said Wheatley mildly. At this, the footman stepped around Wheatley to reach the front door, closed it gently this time, and turned back to the detective.

"If you will wait here," he said moving towards a door leading from the entrance hall, adding "*Sir*," just late enough for it to be an insult. Then he disappeared, leaving Wheatley still holding his bowler.

Sir Toby Hughes-Lewthwaite was a florid, stout man dressed in a tweed suit that, although it was of quality, had seen better days. Frayed shirt-cuffs protruded from his sleeves as he held out his hand in the small drawing room into which the returning footman had escorted the detective.

"Wheatley sir, Detective Wheatley, Brighton Municipal Constabulary," said Wheatley, hiding his surprise that a nobleman should wish to shake hands with him and doing his best to grip the baronet's hand firmly. This was easier said than done. Sir Toby's handshake was limp, his fingers almost clawed. Afterwards, he peered at his hand quizzically, then raised his eyes to Wheatley.

"Cronin sent you, did he?"

"Yes sir, about your niece's disappearance."

"You *are* from Brighton?

"Yes, sir, based at the Town Hall. Now about—"

"Not your work man, your Lodge."

"My lodgings...? Well, Hove actually." Wheatley was thoroughly confused about the way the conversation was going. What had the location of his digs to do with the girl's disappearance? But at least Sir Toby seemed happier at his answer.

"Hove, eh? Well, that explains it, I suppose. Different town, different practices. But all still seeking the path, eh?"

"I certainly have to seek for answers in my profession, sir, yes."

For some reason Sir Toby found this answer extremely funny.

"Quite right, quite right," he brayed. "Mum's the word, eh? Now, what were you saying?"

"About your niece, sir," said Wheatley, relieved to have got the interview back on track.

"Wretched girl. Got home Monday night and she wasn't here. Just left. Disappeared."

"Which?" asked Wheatley.

"Which?"

"Did she leave, in which case, was it a premeditated act? Did she, for example, take any luggage with her? Or did she disappear without trace?"

"You seem to be making it damned complicated. All I know is she's gone."

"So you don't know if she took anything with her. Perhaps if I could look in her room, sir?"

"Her room? Hardly appropriate is it, detective, a young lady's bedroom?" Sir Toby was shaking his head at the idea.

"In that case, perhaps I could have a word with her maid?"

"Well, we really don't go in for that sort of thing. Skeleton staff, you know. I suppose you could talk to Jane, the kitchen maid. Well, come to think of it, the only maid. Jane has been asked to help out if my niece Stephanie needed help with any of those feminine fripperies. I'll get Garson to take you to her." Sir Toby was heading for a bell-pull hanging beside the small, unlit fireplace but Wheatley moved to stop him.

"Just a couple more questions first, please, sir. You told the inspector that she was last seen wearing…" Wheatley put his hat down on a chair and pulled both his notebook and the piece of paper the inspector had given him from the inside pocket of his overcoat, "…a blue day-dress, fur-trimmed waist-length cloak in black velvet and an ostrich feather hat with veil."

"Yes, so?"

"Well sir, if you were out when she left and you haven't inspected her room to see what she has taken, how did you know what she was wearing?"

Sir Toby looked at Wheatley confusedly. "Dashed if I know, the servants must have told me."

"So the servants saw her go?"

"I presume so, you'll have to ask them. Now if you don't mind," he said, yanking the bell-pull, "I need to get on."

Sir Toby escorted him through the sitting room door and then disappeared into the depths of the house, leaving Wheatley once again in the hallway with the uncooperative footman, Garson.

*

"No use at all," he complained to Edwards later in the Detective Office. "Just a series of 'Don't know, sir' and 'I couldn't possibly say, sir'."

"What did the girl, Jane, have to say?" asked Edwards.

"Didn't get to see her, Garson said she 'wasn't available,' whatever that means."

"Did you bung him?"

"Did I what?" said Wheatley.

"I'll take that as a 'No'." Edwards sighed dramatically. "Bung him. Make it worth his while. Slip him a shilling. Really, Wheatley, don't you know how to deal with servants?"

"Well, I've never had any," said Wheatley. "Are they different from other witnesses?"

"That's the point, Wheatley, they're paid *not* to witness. So, what's your next step?"

Wheatley told him.

*

It was bitterly cold despite grey clouds covering the sky. Not a star in sight, the moon just a faint glow and the grass beginning to show the whiteness of frost. Wheatley considered tying his muffler across his head and under his chin to relieve the tingle of his frozen ears, but having formed a mental picture of what he would look like with a scarf round his head and his bowler balanced on top, had settled for blowing on his hands and then placing them over his ears to warm them. He was stationed opposite number 28, Grand Parade on the Steyne. Having gleaned that Sir Toby went out most evenings, Wheatley had wondered whether the niece would take advantage of that and return for some possession or other. It was, he admitted, a bit of a desperate tactic but he had no other leads and Edwards had seemed keen on the plan, telling Wheatley to make sure he was there until after ten o'clock for some reason.

He had arrived after dark. There was a streetlight close to the entrance of the house but the Steyne gardens had many established trees and Wheatley had taken up his watch from the darkness beneath the boughs of a particularly magnificent elm. At seven of the clock, judging by the chimes from the nearby St Peter's Church, he had watched a hansom draw up outside the house and a dapper Sir Toby, old tweeds discarded, now resplendent in evening dress, top hat, cape and cane, whisked off towards the town. Shortly afterwards, the basement door opened and the footman Garson left the house with a rotund woman of about his age. They had set off across the Steyne, gossiping together. Wheatley wondered if the woman was Jane, the all-purpose maid, but decided she was far too old to still be a maid and far too stout to be constantly running up and down the stairs of the five storeys of the house.

Since then the dwelling had been dark and quiet and Wheatley, who estimated that he had spent at least a couple of hours observing nothing, was growing colder by the minute. He was just considering whether to call it a night, even though it was still before Edward's suggested ten p.m., when he noticed a faint flickering light coming from the basement. Stealthily he crossed the road and by crouching down and peering through the railings he was able to see in through the basement window. A girl was crossing the room to place a stub of candle onto the table occupying the centre before walking to the sink to wipe her hands. For a moment Wheatley wondered whether his cold wait had borne fruit and here was the elusive niece, but his excitement withered as he realised that this person was far too young, no more than eighteen or nineteen he estimated, and dressed in the black dress and once-white pinny of a servant. *The elusive Jane,* thought Wheatley as she left the sink carrying a collection of cutlery which she dropped onto the table. She disappeared into the gloom at the back of the kitchen for a second or two, returning with a rag and a tin of polish, and sitting at the table, picked up a spoon and set to cleaning it. Wheatley was just wondering whether to knock at the basement door and hope the girl answered when he became aware of voices approaching. Not wanting to be caught peering through a window at a young woman like a Peeping Tom, he quickly made his way back to the shelter of the darkness beneath the elm tree's boughs.

The voices came closer, crossing the Steyne and passing close to Wheatley who shrank back into the darkness. There were three voices, two men and a woman, and the men's voices were familiar. Looking out,

Wheatley was not surprised to see the footman from that morning's visit and the stout lady who had set out with him that evening. But most unexpectedly, they were accompanied by Detective Edwards.

"Nice drop of beer at the King and Queen. Wery nice. Our thanks for your hospitality, Mr Edwards," Garson was saying, adding, "and this is where we must leave you."

"Afraid not," said Detective Edwards. Then, in a louder voice, he called, "You there, Wheatley?"

"Here," said Wheatley, stepping forward to join the trio at the top of the steps to the basement.

"Him!" Garson quivered, "He's a filthy copper."

"Now then," interjected Edwards, "I'll thank you not to be rude to my colleague."

"Your colleague?" Garson sounded confused. "You told me you worked in the basement of the Town Hall. I thought you was a stoker or something. You mean to say you lied to me?"

"I'll not have that," said Edwards. "I told you I worked in the basement of the Town Hall, yes. And under the Town Hall is…?" There was a moment of befuddlement before the woman piped up.

"The police station," she said.

"Thank you, Mrs Garson, yes, the police station," said Edwards, "and that's where we work. Now then, Detective Wheatley here needs some information about the young lady who's gone missing and he is going to get it this evening, understand? Now, after you." Edwards motioned towards the basement steps. With Mrs Garson in the lead, her husband muttering behind her and the two detectives following, they descended and entered the house. *So this time I* do *have to go in via the tradesman's entrance*, mused Wheatley.

They entered a warm, dimly lit kitchen. The table dominated the centre of the room. A kitchen range set into the chimney breast opposite the window supplied the warmth, an iron pot bubbling on the hotplate. Beneath the window was a sink and draining board, while to the side stood a substantial dresser with assorted cups hanging from its shelves, its plate-rack full of mismatched crockery. Through an archway Wheatley could just make out a scullery and two doors. One door containing a mesh insert was presumably the larder, and the other probably led to the back yard. The maid sitting at the table cleaning the cutlery muttered, "About time." Then, looking up, she dropped the knife she was holding as she saw the two strange men enter.

"Don't you worry yourself, girl," said Mrs Garson, crossing the kitchen and taking up a cloth, using it to pick up the pot from the range which she placed on a trivet at the end of the table. "They're just a couple of coppers come to ask about that fancy piece that's gone missing."

This did little to reassure the maid, it seemed, as she stood up suddenly, knocking over the tin of polish in the process. She was looking around worriedly so that Wheatley, who was watching the trickle of liquid from the tin of Needham's Polishing Paste swirl across the table, had little time to consider Mrs Garson's turn of phrase before moving to stand in front of the door which seemed to lead to the rest of the house. He was pleased to see that Edwards had remained blocking the outside door.

"Sit down, please, miss," said Wheatley. "There's nothing to fear. And could you please light the gas, Mrs Garson? It's awfully dark in here."

"I'll light a couple more candles, detective," she said, reaching for a spill from the container on the dresser. This she lit from the cooker, then used it to light two candles set in brass candlesticks on the mantle-shelf over the range. "The gas was cut off when his lordship's excuses for not paying the bill ran out."

"And the water," said the maid. "I has to queue up at the public pump every morning with a couple of buckets. Bleeding heavy they are, too."

"You be quiet, girl!" Garson slammed his hand flat on the table making the cutlery jump and clatter. "We need to remember our place. Sir Toby is master here and his business is not to be laid bare for the hoi-polloi to gossip about."

"Don't you be getting on your high horse, Micah Garson, he don't pay our wages." Mrs Garson had drawn herself to her full height, placed her fists on her hips and had her eyes fixed on her husband who was visibly wilting before her gaze. "*And* he leaves us short-handed, expecting us to take up the slack. He don't deserve nothing from us."

"Sir Toby doesn't pay your wages?"

It was Edwards who answered Wheatley's question. "Mr and Mrs Garson and Millie are employed by the

35

agency who let the house for the season," he explained. "Typically tenants bring their own servants to make up the full complement, usually a butler, lady's maid and a cook."

"But Sir Toby didn't?"

It was a cowed Garson who answered, "No one."

This was augmented by his wife who added, "Leaving us to do two jobs each, so you ask away, detective." Here she paused to glare at her husband before continuing, "I'm sure we'll *all* give you our full co-operation from now on."

"Thank you, Mrs Garson. Of course I'll want to speak mainly to the last person who saw Miss Stephanie leave. But firstly, who's Millie?"

"I am," said the maid, sitting at the table, "Cheek! What you think I am, a ghost?"

"But I thought you were Jane."

Millie/Jane just folded her arms and sighed so once again it was left to Edwards to explain. "Sir Toby just calls her that. All the posh lot do it — give maid-servants the same name according to their duties. Maids are always coming and going, so when one maid leaves and a new one arrives, they just carry on with the same name. Saves the toffs having to remember a different name every time."

"Yeah, I was Susan last year," said Millie/Jane.

"But Mr and Mrs Garson have retained their name, or are you called something else, too?" asked Wheatley.

"No, them's our names," replied Garson.

"Probably means the master don't have no footman or under-cook at home, wherever that is," added Mrs Garson.

"I quite liked Susan," said Millie/Jane/Susan. "A lot better than 'plain Jane' anyhow."

Wheatley had had quite enough of the confusing world of servants. He had naturally removed his bowler hat upon entering the house and now he placed it onto the table. He reached into his jacket, withdrew his notebook and groped in his overcoat for a stub of pencil.

"Quite so," he said, licking his pencil lead in anticipation. "Now which of you saw Miss Stephanie leave on the day in question?"

This seemingly simple inquiry was met with a baffled silence.

"Do you mean to say none of you saw her leave?"

"Perhaps Sir Toby…"

"Sir Toby told me to question you," Wheatley interrupted, dropping his notebook on the table in frustration. "So if you didn't see her go, how did you know what she was wearing?"

"She always wore the blue day dress," offered Millie.

"Or the grey one," added Mrs Garson thoughtfully before continuing "and she didn't have no winter coat, just a thin summer thing, so the cape was the warmest thing she had."

"And she loved that hat with an ostrich feather," said Millie.

Garson was looking from one to the other of the women as if watching a strenuous game of battledore and seeming to decide that he needed to reassert his authority by saying something, added, "And it was pelting down all day, so she must have worn galoshes over them flimsy shoes of hers."

After this, there was a second or so of uneasy silence as the servants looked anywhere but at the two detectives. Wheatley retrieved his notebook, and taking a calming breath, continued. "So no one saw her leave. She was reported as missing on Tuesday, so who was the last to see her before then?" Again there was silence and the avoidance of eye contact, causing Wheatley to say, "Surely someone saw her Monday? If not, when was the last time you *did* see the young lady?"

"We all go to church on Sunday. Sir Toby insists on it," said Garson eventually.

"So you all went to church together on Sunday?"

"Not together exactly," said Garson. "We goes to the reform chapel on Edward Street, but Sir Toby, he's high church and he and his niece goes to St George's where the old queen used to go."

"Out Kemp Town way," added Mrs Garson.

"And did you see them leave?" asked Wheatley.

"Yes, sir, left in a hansom in time for the ten o'clock service," confirmed Garson.

"We has to wait until the master's gone before we can leave," added Mrs Garson.

Wheatley at last had a fact to write in his notebook, which he did before saying, "And when did they return?"

"Couldn't say, sir," said Garson. As Wheatley glared and Edwards bunched his fists he quickly added, "They didn't return straight away. Sir Toby has his own key and we was so busy here in the kitchen we didn't notice them come in."

"More likely having a crafty kip while the master's away," broke in Edwards, but Garson continued, "They must have come in because Sir Toby rang for tea about five and then went out as usual about seven."

"Tea for two?"

"No, and he went out alone. But that's not unusual. The young lady often retires to her bedroom early."

Wheatley turned to the maid. "How about you, Millie? Did you see the young lady Sunday evening? Did she ring to get you to help her undress for example?"

"No, detective, sorry. She only ever wants my help if she needs to get tarted up to go to some posh do with the master. And that hasn't happened since the Season ended."

"So," Wheatley summarised, "no one has seen Miss Stephanie since Sunday morning, and the description of the clothes she was wearing is only your best guess?"

"That's about it." Millie grinned. She seemed to have got over her initial fright and now gave every sign of enjoying the drama.

"Did you actually check?" Wheatley followed up. "In her wardrobe, for example?"

"No one never told me to," said Millie, her grin slipping.

"Then I think we should do that right now, don't you?" said Wheatley. "If you'd be kind enough to show me the way, Millie. Edwards, you'll stay here?"

Edwards nodded his agreement while the maid went to a cupboard next to the range and removed a candleholder, fitted one of the candles from the mantlepiece into it and made towards the door where Wheatley was standing.

"One moment," said Wheatley. He replaced his notebook and pencil in his jacket and reaching into one of his overcoat pockets withdrew a police-issue lantern. This he opened and lit the burner using another of the spills from the dresser. Closing the lantern door caused a bright light to spring from the lens. "That's better," he said, taking up the lantern.

"Afraid of coming upstairs with me in the dark, detective?" said Millie as she led the way out of the kitchen.

As they entered the first-floor bedroom, Wheatley caught a whiff of musky perfume with an underlying acrid odour that he couldn't quite identify. Directly opposite the door was a window, its curtains tied back, with a dressing table in front, a large wardrobe to the left and a chest to the right. The chimney breast was on the left-hand wall, the grate empty. On the right was a large bed, and on a table next to the bed, Wheatley was pleased to see an ancient oil lamp which Millie proceeded to light.

"There's no fire laid. Is that usual?" he asked.

"No one asked me to. I don't lay no fires less I'm asked. Got enough to do, don't go around looking for work."

Wheatley let Millie's petulance go. He had already opened the wardrobe and was noting the contents.

Day dress, one, grey.
Blouses, two, one white, one cream.
Lady's suit (skirt with matching jacket), one, navy blue.
Evening dresses, two, one white, one gold.
Evening slippers, one pair, pale green.
Court shoes, one pair, brown.

On top of the wardrobe were two hatboxes, one empty, one with a simple black hat such as any young woman would wear during the day.

"No blue day dress," mused Wheatley.

Millie had come to stand next to the detective and had seemingly got over her pique.

"She always liked wearing something demure to church. Either a blouse and skirt or the blue dress. The blue one buttons up higher than that one," she said, pointing to the grey dress, "and a lot higher than them," indicating the evening dresses. Wheatley was no student of ladies' fashion but even he could see that the evening dresses would display as much of the wearer as they concealed.

"Doesn't seem a lot of clothing. Anything else missing?"

"Just her black boots and her cape," said Millie. "And no, she never seemed to have many clothes."

"What about the coat Mrs Garson mentioned, and the galoshes?"

"They're kept in the hall. I can check later if you like."

"Any sign of a suitcase or carpet bag?"

"Not never seen one," answered Millie.

They moved on to the chest of drawers where Millie said the young lady kept her 'necessaries'. On top was a jug and bowl. A neatly folded washing cloth and towel and a bar of Pear's soap in a china soap dish sat next to them. The jug was empty, the cloth, towel and soap dry. Wheatley was just about to ask the maid about the arrangements for hot water when Millie took it on herself to begin opening drawers and displaying the 'necessaries'. It only took a glance at the embarrassing display of linens, cotton and silks as each drawer was opened for Wheatley's inspection to cause him to move on rapidly to the dressing table. On top was a standard triple mirror with a cheap necklace or two strung from the supports, a hairbrush, comb and hand mirror, various pots of cosmetics and powder. Two silver-topped spray bottles stood to the side of the mirror, one containing the musky perfume he had detected on entering the room, the other a lighter scent. In front was a tray containing hair-pins, ear clips, a few brooches and a brass key. The single drawer contained an assortment of sturdy hatpins, ribbons, garters, a buttonhook and the identification of the acrid smell — mothballs.

The bed was neatly made, sheets and blankets tucked in, the eiderdown atop of them unwrinkled. The chamber pot beneath was empty and clean. Wheatley picked up *Everybody's Best Friend*, a book that had been lying face down on the table next to the old oil lamp. It had been opened to the section 'Pitfalls for the Unwary' which followed the chapters on 'Etiquette for All Occasions' and 'How to Develop a Personality'. Smiling as he replaced it, Wheatley noted that the book's opening paragraphs were entitled 'Love and Courtship Problems'.

He returned his attention to the bed. There was a bolster across the head and two pillows side by side. On top of the pillow nearest to him was a square of apricot fabric, which when he picked it up, turned out to be an embroidered shift of finely woven, sheer material.

"Don't think that's your colour," said Millie, taking it from him. Then, before folding and replacing the nightdress on the pillow, she draped it across herself cooing, "How do you think I'd look in this, detective?"

Wheatley turned hastily away, cursing her for giggling at him and himself for the colour that he could feel flooding to his cheeks. He found himself facing the fireplace and for the first time noticed a door in the wall to the left of the chimney breast. The door had been in shadow and was painted to blend in with the wall. Assuming it to be a cupboard, Wheatley tried to open it but found it locked. Remembering and fetching the key from the dressing table tray, he was pleased to find that it fitted and turned easily. He found on opening the door not the cupboard he had been expecting but just the thickness of the wall and another door.

"That's the connecting door," said Millie.

"Connecting to what?" Wheatley asked.

"To the master's room, of course. Now we'd better get back downstairs quick or my reputation will be in ruins, up here at night with a strange man."

So saying, Millie extinguished the oil lamp, picked up her candle and smugly left the room, leaving Wheatley to retrieve his lantern and follow after.

"Wednesday, by the way," Millie said as they entered the kitchen.

"Wednesday?" said Wheatley.

"My day off. Wednesday, once a fortnight between ten and four," she replied.

*

"Thank you for helping me out, Edwards. I've certainly got a lot to learn about interviewing servants." The two detectives were standing under the lamp-post outside of the house.

"You're welcome, Wheatley, we all have to learn. Nostalgic for me. Me old mum and dad were in service, spent all of my early life below stairs." For a moment, Wheatley thought he could see a tear forming in the eye of the usually dour detective, but he should have known better. Edwards continued, "By the way, you owe me five and a tanner."

"A crown?" said Wheatley.

"And sixpence. For the beer. King and Queen's a pricey pub, you know. And the gin. My gawd, that Mrs Garson can put away her gin."

"Oh, right." Wheatley pushed his hand into his pocket which he knew contained just two silver thruppences and a penny ha'penny. Wondering how to explain the shortfall, he looked up to find Edwards grinning down at him.

"Don't trouble yourself, Wheatley, I told the landlord I'd have to report him for watering his beer and he bunged me ten bob to keep quiet."

"Oh, good," said a momentarily relieved Wheatley, then, as an afterthought followed up with, "Is that legal?"

Edwards just shook his head, turned away and called "Goodnight, detective," as he strode purposefully in the direction of the sea front.

"Edwards," called Wheatley after him, "how did you know the landlord watered his beer?"

Edwards kept walking but called back over his shoulder, "Really, Wheatley! *All* landlords water their beer."

"You said five shillings and sixpence."

Wheatley had raided his post office savings account that morning. He placed two half crowns and two threepenny bits on the desk where Detective Edwards was sitting. Edwards stared at the coins confusedly.

"I told you last night, all covered," he said.

"Yes, well, I don't exactly feel comfortable about that."

"Comfortable about what?"

"Well, er, the method of obtaining the payment."

Edwards looked even more confused.

"It was dishonest," blurted Wheatley. "Isn't that what we're about, preventing dishonesty?"

"Well, if you put it like that," Edwards pursed his lips, "that's exactly what I was doing. Preventing a dishonest landlord from watering his beer and defrauding poor innocent punters."

"Yes, but you didn't arrest the man, you took an honorarium," said Wheatley.

"And spent it on beer," he added.

Edwards sighed, looked down at the money, pushed it towards Wheatley, sighed again and said, "Number one, I was off duty. Number two, if I had arrested the landlord, he would have been fined more than the ten bob anyway. Also he'd have lost his licence and had his pub shut. You'd have had to fork out five and six and I'd be four and a tanner worse off." Edwards paused for breath, then continued. "Now, if we arrested one, we'd have to arrest them all. And if we arrested them all, every pub in Brighton would be shut and we'd have riots on our hands. Did you think of that?"

"Well, no, but…"

"No buts, Wheatley, time's getting on and you're going to need that," here he nodded at the money, "if you're going to treat your piece."

"My piece?"

"That little maid from last night. Don't tell me you haven't taken her up on her offer?"

"Well, I did send her a postcard suggesting we meet for tea this afternoon," admitted Wheatley, colouring slightly. "Only to obtain information about the case of course."

"Of course." Edwards grinned. "Where are you taking her?"

"I thought the tea shop on the corner of St James' Street."

"Joe Lyons, eh? The Cornerhouse no less. Well, you're going to need this there." So saying, Edwards picked up the two half crowns and two thruppences, opened Wheatley's right hand and placed the coins in it. "Now get going," he said. "Don't want to keep the little lady waiting."

*

"What I don't understand," said Wheatley, "is why no one seems bothered about the disappearance."

They were sitting at a really quite pleasant table towards the back of the restaurant, the window tables being reserved for more affluent guests. Millie had just drawn breath to respond when a waitress arrived and began to fuss with cups and saucers, a second waitress behind her setting down a milk jug and sugar bowl. Once the servers had retreated, Millie seemed to have lost her enthusiasm to comment and so the detective began again.

"What I mean is…" was as far as he got before the waitresses returned, one placing a teapot and hot water container on the table, handles carefully angled towards Millie, while the other added jam, clotted cream and a small plate containing thin slices of lemon. Wheatley was about to continue when Millie held up her hand to silence him, giggling as the waitresses approached yet again. One placed a heavily laden three-tiered contraption in the centre of the table, and the other provided clean plates and cutlery. They then both stood back as if to admire their handiwork.

"Will that be all, sir?" the first server asked. Wheatley had formed an answer and was about to deliver it when he noticed that having asked the question, both waitresses had bobbed in a cursory curtsey and turned away without waiting for a reply.

"Don't it look lovely?" enthused Millie. Wheatley gazed at the tea stand, taking in the bottom layer of incredibly thin crustless sandwiches, the cream cakes in the centre, the scones — two plain, two speckled with fruit — on the top and calculated that he would need most of the five and six he was still determined to return to Edwards to pay for probably the most expensive cup of tea he had ever had.

"Now, about the disappearance," said Wheatley.

"Milk or lemon?" said Millie.

The etiquette of tea seemed interminable with Millie taking complete charge and Wheatley having to answer so many questions. One lump or two? Ham or cucumber? Jam or cream first, and of course, with or without currants? Eventually though, after Millie's exertions and her third cream cake, she looked up and smiled. Taking this for permission to continue his investigation, Wheatley again asked about the apparent lack of concern about Miss Stephanie's disappearance.

"It's not as if we're family servants," Millie said. "We tend to different people every season, and let me tell you, someone taking off is mild compared with some of the goings-on we see."

"Yes, I suppose so." Wheatley frowned. "But Sir Toby seems very unconcerned. After all, she is his niece."

"Oh, him," said Millie, giving Wheatley what he took to be a knowing look. "I think he was fed up with her."

"Or her, him," she added before the detective could ask further. "I think it was the key that did it."

"The key?" asked Wheatley.

"Yes, the key you found in her dressing table tray. I don't know where she got it, but lately she's been using it to lock herself in her bedroom of an evening."

"Both doors," she added.

Wheatley was just about to ask for the significance of Millie's statement when he became aware that they were being approached.

"Almost didn't see you back here in the gloom," said Edwards. "Didn't you tell them you was a copper? Always get a window table that way."

"Edwards," said Wheatley. "We were talking about…"

"Miss," said Edwards, touching the brim of his bowler and inclining his head towards Millie. "Sorry to interrupt this tête-à-tête, detective, but we've got a body."

*

The Sussex County Hospital sits on the side of a hill overlooking the English Channel. Brighton's mortuary occupies the basement dug into the chalk, accessed through a pair of unmarked doors on the outside of the hospital building. As the two detectives descended the ramp, feeling the cold dampness wafting up from below and breathing in its sweet carbolic smell, Wheatley's mind was on Millie's parting words outside of the teashop; *"Next week, same time then. I should have weekly days off now Sir Toby has left,"* and wondering why he hadn't enquired further about the disappearance of another member of the household. So much so that he almost missed Edwards' information about the body.

"…On the beach under the new pier," he was finishing as Wheatley stopped dead.

"When did you say the body was discovered?"

"Tuesday morning, I told you."

"But that was over two days ago! How come we're only just hearing about it?"

"I don't suppose anyone thought it important. Bodies are regularly washed up on the beach." Edwards had continued descending and was now waiting in front of a pair of swing doors, painted red but heavily indented with scuff marks at waist height. "You're lucky we heard at all. It was only because some of the lads was saying about the drowned young woman with the big…" Here Edwards cupped his hands in front of his chest, grinning, then as if suddenly realising where he was and what he was saying, dropped them and finished lamely, "Well, as I say, lucky I heard," and disappeared through the swing doors.

As Wheatley followed, a chill settled around him and the smell of disinfectant, overlaid with a sickly sweetness, assaulted his nostrils.

"Bit grim, isn't it? Your first time here?" asked Edwards. Wheatley just nodded. The two detectives were standing in a clear space containing an unoccupied desk. The wall behind the desk was dominated by a long window with curtains drawn across it. Another set of the red-painted double doors were to the left of the window.

Wheatley wondered whether these led to the outside but if that was the case, why were the curtains excluding the daylight? He returned his attention to the desk where a bell such as one might see on the reception counter of an hotel stood, along with a hand-written notice 'Ring for Attenshun'. The area was lit dimly by an oil lamp suspended above the desk, one of a series which hung from the arched brick roof forming a corridor disappearing into the darkness to the detectives' left. About halfway along, other arched entrances could be seen branching off from the central walkway.

"Well, I suppose we'd better…" Edwards nodded at the desk. Wheatley stepped forward and hovered his hand over the bell, pausing and taking a deep breath, which he instantly regretted, before dropping his hand onto the plunger. A loud 'ding' echoed around the walls and Wheatley hastily withdrew his hand. For a moment nothing happened. Then, to the sound of footsteps, and incongruously, a high tenor voice singing 'Rock of Ages,' a figure appeared from one of the side entrances off the central corridor and approached the two detectives. As it drew nearer, the singing stopped and the figure began speaking.

"Sorry, gents, the necroscopy was completed this morning, too late, I'm afraid."

Wheatley and Edwards didn't quite know what to make of this. Before them stood a short but portly man, bulked by the mass of clothing he was wearing, presumably to keep out the chill. A long scarf over which straggled his sparse locks and a brown porter's coat completed his outfit. The man had begun rooting about in the scarf at the back of his neck, pulling something forth which he examined quizzically, then flicked away before adding, "Though there are a few tasty cadavers you might wish to view for a shilling."

After the man had been disabused of his assumption that the two detectives were macabre voyeurs and having been appraised of the purpose for their visit, he had introduced himself as "Mr Shadrach Mears, mortuary assistant," before moving to the swing doors in the wall behind the desk and asking Wheatley and Edwards to follow him. The doors led not to the outside as Wheatley had thought, but to a room which burst into light as the assistant turned a switch on the wall. The room was a revelation. Unlike the medieval look of the rest of the mortuary, this room was a wonder of modernity. The walls were fully tiled, dark green to the midpoint, bright white above. The rear wall had a deep polished wood counter at waist level with a sink set into it, tap above and drawer units below. The floor was concrete sealed with red paint and in the centre of the room stood a stout table, its top completely covered in gleaming copper. But the biggest surprise was the lighting. Dangling from the ceiling, three cables held three glowing globes which gave a stark bright light. The modern wonder of electricity!

The detectives had little time to admire this temple to modernity. The mortuary attendant had left them in the room and a crash heralded his return. He was pushing a trolley containing what was unmistakably a shrouded body. Parking the trolley parallel to the table, Mears slid his arms under the torso and looked towards Edwards.

"Give me a hand then," he said, nodding towards the feet.

"Right," said Edwards after a brief hesitation, and between them the two men lifted the burden onto the table. Mears proceeded to straighten the body, untucking the shroud and fussily ensuring that it hung equally from the edges of the table. Then, with a showman-type flourish, he whipped the covering sheet back, and folding it neatly at the waist, stated "There you are, gentlemen." As he left, pushing the empty trolley back through the doors, he added, "You realise I'll have to polish that bloody table again when you leave." The doors slammed behind him and the strains of 'Jerusalem' started up, at first *fortissimo* then fading away as the sounds of Mears' footsteps receded.

It was not the first dead body that Wheatley had seen but it was the first that had undergone a necroscopy and he took some time to take in the disturbing sight of the hastily sutured Y-shaped scar which began at the collar bones, converged at the sternum and disappeared beneath the sheet covering the lower part of the body. Mastering his discomfort, Wheatley lifted the sheet to cover the poor girl but was stopped by Edwards saying, "Well, it looks like the lads at the station were right." Mistaking Wheatley's silence for incomprehension he added, "About her..." nodding towards the body before lapsing into silence as

Wheatley stared at him in disbelief. "Just trying to lighten the mood," Edwards muttered a second later. The awkward tableau of Edwards eyeing the floor in embarrassment, Wheatley still staring at him and shaking his head whilst holding the shroud aloft was interrupted by the sound of the door opening and a woman's voice saying, "Can I help you, gentlemen?"

The voice belonged to a tall, handsome woman, the grey tinging her auburn hair placing her in her early to mid-forties. Her face was heavily freckled with some of the speckles disappearing into the lines radiating from her eyes. She was wearing a navy-blue dress and a pristine white starched apron, but without the frilly cap Wheatley would expect a nurse to wear. She carried a folder which she put down before taking the sheet from Wheatley's hand and settling it over the body, leaving just the head and neck showing.

"You are here about the necroscopy?" she asked, opening one of the drawers and removing a wooden block. This she placed under the body's neck before pulling the girl's dark hair back.

"She didn't drown, then," said Edwards, gazing at the livid abrasion around the neck revealed by the drawing back of the hair. The woman picked up the folder she had brought into the room with her and handed it silently to Edwards. He glanced at it briefly, then handed it to Wheatley without opening it. "I suppose the…" — here he ran his index finger across his throat — "was the reason for the report."

"Not really," said the woman, moving to the back of the room where she opened one of the many drawers beneath the counter and took out a long strip of fur. "She had this wrapped around her throat when she was brought here. It was only when we were preparing the body that the neck abrasions came to light. No, the coroner ordered the necroscopy to establish cause of death. Usually he doesn't bother with bodies washed up on the beach, but perhaps he saw the quality of this one's clothing." Here she indicated the still open drawer before replacing the strip of fur.

Wheatley looked up from reading the report.

"Was she washed up?" he asked. "No mention of water in the lungs in here."

"And no salt staining to the clothing," answered the woman. "No, I think she was abandoned there in the hope that your colleagues would assume just another drowning."

Wheatley had gone back to reading the report.

"It says cause of death, Syncope," said Wheatley. "I think I need assistance here. The necroscopy report is signed by a Dr B. Buchanan. Any chance we could have a word with him?"

"Absolutely no chance you could talk to him," said the woman. Then, after a short silence she added, "But I dare say you could have a word with *her*."

There was another moment of silence before Edwards blurted out, "Blimey, a lady doctor, *here.*"

"Do you address male doctors as gentlemen doctors?" came a sharp reply.

"No," said Edwards. "Of course not."

"Then kindly afford me the same courtesy," said the woman. "Perhaps we should introduce ourselves? Barbara Buchanan, M.D., at your service. And you are?"

After the introductions, Dr Buchanan began to explain that there were only three official causes of death for a coroner's report: syncope, asphyxia and coma. She was interrupted by Detective Edwards, who had been looking increasingly uncomfortable.

"Excuse me, doctor, but this is more Wheatley's cup of tea than mine, so to speak." Turning to Wheatley, Edwards said, "We have a body that matches the description, but we need a positive identification. How about I go and arrange that with Sir Toby while you go through the mumbo jumbo with the doctor here?"

"If you wish," said Wheatley. "But I don't think you'll find Sir Toby at home. Millie said he'd left."

Edwards did a double take.

"When? How? Really, Wheatley, fancy springing that on me now."

"I don't know any more than that. Millie only mentioned it as we were leaving the teashop."

"All the more reason for me to go visit that house again," said Edwards, nodding. "I can get one of the servants to identify the body. I dare say Garson might do it. Probably want paying, though. Would eight o'clock tomorrow morning be convenient, Doctor?"

"I'll ask Shadrach to arrange it," confirmed the doctor.

"And I'll get to the bottom of this Sir Toby leaving business with your sweetheart, Wheatley" added Edwards as he departed.

"She's not my sweetheart," blustered Wheatley, but he was only addressing a swinging door.

Dr Buchanan raised a single eyebrow, and said, "Well, if we are to address this 'mumbo jumbo,' detective, perhaps we could retire to my office?"

Dr Buchanan's 'office' turned out to be the Snug Bar of the Sudeley Arms on the corner of a street opposite the hospital's main entrance. As she ushered Wheatley through the crowded public bar and into the Snug, he noticed a few smiles and nods in their direction, balanced by the turning of many more backs. They settled at a table beneath a frosted mirror advertising Tamplin's Ales and Wheatley noticed that the barman had followed them in. He placed a large brandy glass in front of Dr Buchanan, then folded his arms and regarded Wheatley.

"This one's a bit young even for you, Doc," he said, then, looking towards Wheatley, "Drink?"

"I'm on duty," said Wheatley, taken aback.

"So are half of them in there," said the barman. "They seem to think that operating half-cut improves their performance."

"Simon," interrupted Dr Buchanan warningly, "don't tease."

"Simon is the barman and chief gossip here," she said to Wheatley. "And Mr Wheatley here is a member of our local constabulary," she added to the barman.

"Lawks, the rozzers are in," hammed Simon. "Everyone on your best behaviour." Then, addressing Wheatley directly, he said, "I've got some nice sarsaparilla behind the bar, I'll bring you a glass," adding as he left the Snug, "I'll pop a smidgin of gin into it for free."

The doctor laughed. "Take no notice, he'll do no such thing, This doubles for the common room at the hospital. Most of the customers work at the Sussex County."

"I couldn't help noticing as you walked in that some of your colleagues seemed less than pleased to see you," said Wheatley.

Dr Buchanan took her glass in both hands, swirled the brandy, inhaled the fumes noisily and finally took a sip of the liquid which she held in her mouth before swallowing with a contented sigh. Smiling, she replaced the glass and said, "I am afraid that many of my colleagues share Detective Edwards' view of the appropriateness of female doctors."

"I'm sure Mr Edwards was just remarking on your place of employment," said Wheatley. "Which you must admit is unusual…" Wheatley's sentence tailed off as he realised what he was saying. Dr Buchanan finished it for him.

"…for a woman," she said.

"Well, unusual for anyone really, necroscopy," Wheatley said lamely.

"I prefer the term pathology," said the doctor. She took another sip of her brandy. "They can't stop us from training, particularly with the women-only medical schools in London and Edinburgh. They couldn't ban me from employment, though many did try," she continued, "and I have to admit it helps having a famous surname."

Wheatley was trying so frantically to think of anyone famous with the name of Buchanan that he missed the next few words and forced himself to refocus as the doctor continued,

"...but it has to be *suitable* employment." Dr Buchanan looked around the small room in silence for a moment. "Yes, suitable employment," she sighed. "And that means children; spoiled brats snivelling all over the place, revolting, not for me. Or women's troubles: even worse." Here she actually shuddered. "Or hide yourself away out of sight of the great and the good."

"So you hid yourself away in the mortuary," said Wheatley.

"Yes, I did a deal. I surrendered my rights to surgical beds in the hospital for the promise that I could perform post-mortems and for a modern pathology laboratory, or 'necroscopic facility' as those in charge refer to it. And it turns out I rather like it. Quiet. Challenging. And the patients don't answer back."

At this point the barman entered, placed a glass of a deep purple liquid down in front of Wheatley and another large brandy in front of the doctor. "Thank you, Simon," she said.

"You're welcome, Doc," he said, then to Wheatley, "No gin, Constable," before turning back to the Public Bar.

"Close the door behind you please, Simon," called Dr Buchanan. "Confidential business."

Simon nodded knowingly and left the bar chuckling, ensuring the door was shut behind him.

Strange reaction, thought Wheatley before saying, "Now about this report, Dr Buchanan."

"Call me Barbara. And I can't go on calling you constable."

"I prefer the term detective."

Barbara smiled. "Constable, detective. What do your friends call you?"

"Wheatley, just Wheatley," said the detective.

The doctor closed her eyes momentarily, then, shaking her head, said, "Well, Just Wheatley, how can I help you?"

"You say the cause of death was syncope, which means I believe a loss of blood?"

"Strictly speaking a failure of circulation, but yes, insufficient blood reaching the heart, resulting in death."

"But there was clear evidence of strangulation, the marks around her neck. Surely that would be asphyxia?"

"It would be if that had been the cause of death, but following the throttling there was some kind of attack which caused internal bleeding. Quite frenzied, in fact. I'm surprised it didn't bring on an abortion."

"Abortion?" interrupted Wheatley.

"Yes. The girl was pregnant, approximately fourteen weeks. It *is* in the report, detective."

"But how?" stammered Wheatley.

61

"I should think the usual method, Wheatley." She looked at him and again he noticed the lift of a single eyebrow. "Shall I carry on?"

Dr Buchanan went on to describe how she imagined the chain of events. The approach of someone the girl trusted — "No sign of a struggle," she attested. The placing of some kind of ligature around the neck from behind — a double loop of something strong and flat about three eighths of an inch wide. "I'm quite sure she would have lost consciousness at this point, but I believe she was still alive. The subsequent stabbing of the lower abdomen resulted in an uncontrolled internal haemorrhage eventually causing heart failure and death. Hence, syncope," she finished.

"You said the attack was frenzied," said Wheatley slowly. "But surely there would have been external evidence obvious when the body was discovered. Extensive blood stains, for instance."

"There were six or seven puncture wounds in the lower abdomen, some shallow, some deep, but all caused by a long thin object. Perhaps the narrow entry wounds restricted bleeding. Or I am wrong, and she was already dead from the throttling. Forensics is far from an exact science. Either way, there was overwhelming evidence of catastrophic internal haemorrhage once I opened the body cavity."

"A long thin object," said Wheatley, feeling slightly queasy as he considered what the doctor was saying. "Like a stiletto? Or the blade of a scissor?"

"No, narrower than both and longer than scissors, more like a long, thin, meat skewer. But whatever it was, it certainly did extreme damage, piercing both the lower aorta and the iliac arteries, notably…" Dr Buchanan went on to describe the evidence excitedly in ever-increasing detail, before suddenly looking up at Wheatley and stopping. "You look pale, detective," she said. She held out her brandy glass. "It's my medical opinion that you need this more than I do."

Wheatley took the drink and downed it, his hands trembling. "Thank you, Barbara," he said as he carefully replaced the empty glass onto the table.

"Now, I think you should go home. We can sort out any further details later."

"Yes, I think I shall."

Moving slowly and carefully Wheatley left the tavern without saying goodbye and decided to walk home along the seafront rather than search for an omnibus. It was a fair distance, but he had a lot of thinking to do and a strong draught of salty sea air would blow away the cobwebs.

Thursday 8th February 1894

"It's obvious isn't it, Wheatley?" said Detective Edwards the next morning. "Sir Toby what's-his-name gets the girl up the duff, gets rid of her, then does a runner. Case solved."

The two detectives were back standing outside of the unmarked doors which formed the entrance to the mortuary at the Sussex County Hospital. Wheatley was still disturbed at the developments in the case but had to admit that Edwards' conclusions seemed logical.

"But his own niece," he said. "How could he?"

Edwards looked at Wheatley quizzically, shook his head and chuckled.

"There's nothing to laugh at," said Wheatley. "This is tragic."

"I wasn't being disrespectful; I was just smiling at you. You do realise this is Brighton, right?"

"What's that got to do with it? Of course I know we're in Brighton."

Wheatley turned away, gazing for a moment across the roofs of Kemp Town to the sea beyond before turning back to his colleague who had placed his hands in his pockets and stood kicking at the ground. Edwards took a deep breath and launched into his explanation.

"Every year people — gentry — come to Brighton for the Season. Many are genuine families enjoying the theatre, concerts, balls and all that posh stuff. But a fair proportion are men who bring their 'nieces' to have fun while their wives and families are left at home." Edwards pulled a hand from his pocket and pointed to his temple. "Think about it, Wheatley. Why do you think that connecting doors between bedrooms are common in the type of house rented by blokes like Sir Toby? All genteel and above board from the outside, but Sodom and Gomorrah inside."

"Miss Stephanie wasn't really his niece?"

"At last the gas is lit," said Edwards, rubbing his hands together. "Now where is our witness? We need to get that body identified officially." Then, looking over Wheatley's shoulder, he continued, "Ah, here she is at last."

"She?" said Wheatley.

"The Garsons weren't too keen about viewing a dead body and I didn't think it mattered who did it as long as someone did," explained Edwards, "so…"

"So I said I'd do it," came a familiar voice and Wheatley spun round to see a smiling Millie standing there.

"A dead body don't bother me. It's just like going to sleep, my dad used to say. Aren't you pleased to see me, detective?"

"Isn't that from Miss Stephanie's bedroom?" was all the startled Wheatley could think of to say, pointing at the hat adorning Millie's head.

"Waste not, want not," said Millie, primping her hair. "When Sir Toby did a flit, he only took his own things and left the rest of the stuff. I just managed to get me hands on this before Micah Garson and that fat wife of his took the lot down Uncle's. Don't you think it suits me?"

Wheatley's head was reeling from the information that valuable evidence was being pawned or misappropriated so that he was still gaping at the maid as Edwards said they'd better get going and he and Millie disappeared through the doors.

Wheatley followed and as he entered the mortuary, he saw Shadrach Mears standing behind the reception desk humming 'For Those in Peril on the Sea', with Edwards and Millie standing in front of him. As Wheatley joined them, Shadrach lifted a finger and continued humming until he had finished the final phrase, then stood looking from one to the other of the two detectives. It seemed to Wheatley that the mortuary attendant had made an effort to improve his appearance. Though retaining his insulating clothing and brown overall, the long scarf was gone, replaced by a clean celluloid collar and black cravat. The reason for his waiting in silence became clear as with ever exaggerated eye movements and nodding he at last got through the message that the detectives should remove their hats. This accomplished he said, "Sorry for your loss, but be comforted that the departed rests in the arms of our

Lord." Then, spreading his hands to indicate the items spread across the desk, he stated, "The deceased's effects."

A pile of clothing was topped by a blue dress. Wheatley noted the care with which the garments had been folded so that any tears or bloodstains were hidden. Next to the pile of clothing were two hair combs, a necklace with a St Christopher medallion, a cheap-looking ring with a green stone and the jagged strip of fur which Dr Buchanan had said was wrapped around the victim's throat when she was first found, all neatly laid out. Adjacent to these stood a clinical-looking metal bowl containing two farthings and a handwritten notice saying 'TIPs'.

"No shoes," mused Wheatley, only realising he had said it aloud when Millie added, "No corset, neither."

Meanwhile, Shadrach had moved to the curtained window behind the desk, and once he had their full attention, theatrically whooshed the curtains open. This would have been dramatic except that the room behind was in darkness and as they approached the window Wheatley, could see only himself, Edwards and Millie reflected in the glass.

"I shall now illuminate the deceased," said Shadrach sonorously and Wheatley felt Millie's hand grip tightly onto his arm. *So much for "a dead body don't bother me,"* he thought. The brightness of the electric lights blinded them for an instant, then Millie gasped, her hand gripping even tighter, and she moved closer to Wheatley so that he could feel the heat of her body pressed against him. He moved slightly to provide a respectable distance between them while using his free hand to pat three times at Millie's hand wrapped around his arm, before returning his attention to the corpse. He was pleased to see that a shroud, pulled up to the chin, maintained decency and obscured her injuries.

After a few moments, Edwards spoke. "Now, miss, will you please identify the body?"

"I'm afraid I can't do that, detective."

"Come along, Millie," said Detective Edwards. "No need to be afraid. Just identify the body as that of Stephanie Hughes-Lewthwaite, late of 28, Grand Parade, Brighton, County of Sussex, sign my bit of paper and we can all go home."

"No, I really can't, detective," said Millie. "You see, that's not her. I've never seen that woman before in my life."

While the two detectives tried to grasp this turn of events, Millie had returned to the desk and was gently stroking the blue dress with the fingers of her left hand.

"This, though," she said. "This *is* Miss Stephanie's. I'd stake me life on it."

Friday 9th February 1894

Wheatley knocked on the Inspector of Detectives' office door and waited. He was about to knock again when he heard "Come," from inside, took a deep breath and entered. Inspector Cronin was, as usual, sitting by the side of a roaring fire, which even on this cold February morning made the room overheated. Unusually, he wasn't reading a newspaper but a police file. The latest report on the disappearance and murder.

"Murder, Watts, terrible business."

"Wheatley, sir," said Wheatley.

"Yes, of course. As I was saying, Whatley, terrible business. This is what comes of courts handing out meagre sentences. An eye for an eye, detective, an eye for an eye." The inspector turned his head and was gazing towards his pristinely empty desk set in front of the window which gave a view across the sea front to the channel beyond. Wheatley was unsure whether he was required to answer and decided to remain silent. This, it seemed, was a wrong decision.

"Well, man, don't just stand there. Progress?"

"Apart from the details in the report, sir, we have little more to add. We have been unable to establish the identity of the victim or the whereabouts of the missing woman."

"Lady, Whatley, the missing lady. There is a difference, you know," interrupted the Inspector.

"Quite, sir, though there is some doubt that…"

"Not interested in doubts, detective, interested in facts. So, what's your next move, eh?"

"Well, sir, Sergeant Johnson has officers checking the pawn shops to see if perhaps the missing lady's dress had been pawned and that was how the victim came by it."

"So, you think the dress might be a coincidence, good thought."

"Not really," answered Wheatley. "The victim was found on Tuesday morning. Miss Stephanie went missing less than thirty-six hours before. Doesn't seem enough time for a coincidence. Far more likely that the victim and the missing lady were acquainted."

While Wheatley had been speaking, Inspector Cronin had gone to his desk, opened a drawer and removed a pipe and tobacco pouch. Returning to his fireside chair, he took time to roll and tamp the tobacco into the pipe bowl, before removing a Vesta case from a pocket of his waistcoat and striking a match. Drawing noisily on the pipe until lit to his satisfaction, he threw the spent match into the fire before exhaling a cloud of smoke. Then, pointing the pipestem at Wheatley, he said, "Don't jump to conclusions too easily, young man. I can't imagine a gentleman of the calibre of Sir Tobias being involved in anything sordid like a murder."

"Yes, about Sir Toby," followed up Wheatley. "You did read that he has also gone missing."

"Missing? I don't think so, Whatley," said the inspector. "Probably gone home to await developments."

"Exactly, sir," said Wheatley. "We have his address so I thought I would go there to interrogate him…"

Wheatley got no further, "Oh no, no, no, Constable. As I said, I can vouch for him as being on the level."

"But he might have valuable evidence, might have seen something. If I could just speak to him," said Wheatley somewhat desperately.

The Inspector thought for a moment. "I suppose we should leave no stone unturned, eh, even if it is a waste of time. London, isn't it? His main residence?"

Wheatley confirmed this, his hopes rising.

"There you are then. Write to the Metropolitan Police Commissioner, explain the circumstances and see if he might organise some discreet enquiries. Off our patch, ceases to be our problem, don't you see? Leave it to the London Police. They will know what to do."

"Sir, I really feel…"

"That will be all, detective."

"Wheatley, sir, Detective Wheatley," said Wheatley as he departed, leaving the Inspector sucking on his pipe and exuding clouds of smoke into the room.

Coughing at the cloud of smoke suddenly blown into his compartment, Wheatley used the leather strap to slam the window closed as the train whistled through the Clayton tunnel. Settling back, he wondered whether his brief career as a detective was over. Edwards had promised to cover for him as best he could, but he was in real trouble if Inspector Cronin found out that Wheatley had disregarded his orders and was now on the 11.13 express to London Victoria.

*

Number 34 Montagu Square was an impressive Georgian house with pristine white stone cladding to the basement and ground floor. The first-floor bay window opened out onto a balcony overlooking the central gardens. Wheatley had taken an omnibus from Victoria Station to Marble Arch, then walked a few minutes north to the Square, which, he noted to himself was definitely not a square, more an elongated oblong. He stood in the gardens for a few moments, observed curiously by a gaggle of nannies airing their charges, opposite the address on Sir Toby Hughes-Lewthwaite's card. After lifting one foot at a time to polish the toecaps of his boots on the rear of his trouser legs, he set out meaningfully across the street, and avoiding the basement stairs to the tradesmen's entrance, knocked determinedly on the front door. The door was opened by a smartly dressed servant who looked quizzically at Wheatley.

"Police," said Wheatley, conveniently forgetting to mention which police force he belonged to. "Detective Wheatley to see Sir Tobias Hughes-Lewthwaite."

"Do you have an appointment, sir?" asked the servant, extremely politely but ensuring that he blocked the entrance with the half-open front door and his considerable bulk.

"I have his card," said Wheatley, drawing his notebook from an inside pocket, taking out the card given to him by Inspector Cronin at the beginning of the investigation and offering it to the servant.

There was a pause, then the servant turned and reached behind himself, re-turning to hold out a small silver tray towards the detective. Wheatley considered for a moment before placing the card face up on the tray. Another pause, then the servant opened the door fully allowing Wheatley to enter into the hallway.

"If you will wait here, sir," he said, "I shall see if the master is at home."

Wheatley stood on the black and white checked hall floor. Ahead of him was an impressive marble staircase, next to it an arch through which the servant had disappeared. To his right was an internal door and a large mirror was fixed to the wall to his left, flanked by a side-table on one side and a coat stand and umbrella rack on the other. He was just checking his appearance in the mirror when the servant returned, saying, "If you will follow me sir." They processed up the stairs to the first-floor landing where the servant opened a door and motioned Wheatley through. He entered what he took to be an empty room, the tick of the Ormolu clock on the mantle-shelf and the crackle of a roaring fire in the grate below the only sounds he could hear. He was in the bay-windowed room on the first floor he had admired from the street below. Crossing towards the window to see how the gardens would look from this height, he heard the distinct sound of a throat being cleared behind him. The fireplace had two tall wing-back armchairs facing in towards the fire and almost subsumed in one of these was an elegantly dressed lady in her fifties observing him through a lorgnette.

"Detective Constable Wheatley," said Wheatley, hastily removing his hat.

"I believe you wish to see my husband," said the woman, evidently Lady Hughes-Lewthwaite. She indicated the other fireside chair with a flick of her lorgnette. "Come and sit down and tell me all about it,"

Wheatley sat gingerly on the edge of the chair's plumped feather cushions, then replied, "It concerns his time in Brighton."

"Brighton?" said the lady.

"Yes, and the disappearance of his niece."

"His niece?"

At this point Wheatley remembered his conversation with Edwards about 'nieces' and wondered if he should have mentioned her as Lady Hughes-Lewthwaite said, "And when was this disappearance, pray?"

Wheatley was feeling very hot at this moment, partly from sitting so close to a roaring fire in his overcoat, and partly from realising that the conversation was not going well. However, he could see no alternative but to carry on, answering, "We believe Lady Stephanie, his... er... your... niece disappeared Sunday last, though Sir Toby, of course, returned yesterday."

"I see," said Lady Hughes-Lewthwaite rising and crossing the room. "I have a telephone call to make, but if you'll wait here, I'll have my husband join you." Wheatley was still struggling to rise from the over-stuffed armchair when she paused to say, "By the way, Constable, my husband and I have no nieces, or nephews for that matter, and we've both been in residence here since we returned from the Continent at the beginning of October," before leaving the room.

Wheatley was trying to make sense of that information when the door opened and a tall man in morning dress entered and said, "Well?"

"Detective Constable Wheatley," said Wheatley, "wishing to speak to Sir Tobias Hughes-Lewthwaite, baronet."

"Well?" said the man again, moving to side-table and ringing a hand bell.

"You're not…? Are you…?" Whoever this man was, he was not the Sir Toby Wheatley had met in Brighton. At that point, the servant who had opened the front door entered the room.

"Cartwright, would you kindly explain to this confused young man who I am and then escort him from the premises."

"Of course, Sir Tobias," said Cartwright. Turning to Wheatley he said, "This is Sir Tobias Hughes-Lewthwaite, Baronet and Justice of the Peace for this Parish." Waiting a few moments while Wheatley stared confusedly from one to the other, he followed this up with, "And now sir, if you will follow me."

As he was escorted to the front step Wheatley suddenly remembered the calling card which was needed as evidence and asked the servant to return it.

"The other gentlemen have that, sir," he said.

"Other gentlemen?" But Wheatley was too late, the front door had been firmly closed behind him.

As he slowly descended the Hughes-Lewthwaite premises wondering whether his day could get any worse, Wheatley became aware of a large man blocking the pavement in front of him. Moving a step to his right to go around him, Wheatley was impeded by the man taking a step to *his* left, causing the detective to halt. Hearing a noise behind him, Wheatley turned to see an even larger man standing directly behind him.

"I think you'd better come with us, sir," said the smaller of the two, "before you cause any more trouble."

The entrance to Marylebone (bizarrely pronounced Marley-bone by his escort) Police Station had been familiar to Wheatley. Same blue lamp hanging at the entrance. Same reception desk with an officer he would swear could be Sergeant Johnson's twin, not by his appearance, perhaps, but certainly by his demeanour. Same cold corridor and hard wooden bench where he was seated and told to wait by the two men who had turned out, to Wheatley's relief, to be detectives from the Metropolitan Police Force rather than the ruffians he at first had taken them for. But now he was in completely alien surroundings. Unlike the cubby-hole he was used to in Brighton, the Marylebone Detective office was a large room on the first floor with windows overlooking Savile Row where carts and carriages jostled, and the occasional automobile roared. There were seven desks in all, six in pairs and a seventh with a telephone occupied by a Detective Sergeant. But it was not this bustling space which was the biggest contrast. At the back of the room was a partition, part panelled, part glazed, which formed the Inspector of Detective's office. Unlike the sparse elegantly furnished office of Inspector Cronin, this office appeared to have been thrown together with mismatched furniture crammed seemingly at random into any nook or cranny. The only similarity with the Brighton Inspector's office was the stuffiness of the room, not caused by a roaring fire but by the heat of two gas lights emerging from the wall to the rear of the office and a pair of oil lamps, all of which supplied the illumination to augment the light from the windows filtered through the glazed portion of the partition. One oil lamp stood on the corner of a large, battered desk which dominated the room. The top of the desk was covered with papers, folders, an empty cup and saucer, a half-eaten sandwich and a pair of boots. Inside of the boots were the feet of Detective Inspector Fisher who was lounging back in his chair holding a sheaf of telegrams in one hand and a business card in the other. And this Inspector was the biggest contrast of all. Needing a shave, his jacket thrown over the back of his chair, his waistcoat unbuttoned and his shirt sleeves rolled to the elbow he could not have been more different to Wheatley's image of an Inspector of Detectives.

Wheatley had been escorted to the Inspector's office by the smaller of the two detectives who had accosted him outside of the Hughes-Lewthwaite residence. As they entered, the Inspector flicked the business card he had been holding at Wheatley saying, "I think this is yours," before dismissing the escort. Wheatley bent to pick it up and saw that it was the visiting card he had used to enter the house on Montagu Square.

As he straightened, Inspector Fisher continued, "Do you know an Inspector Cronin, Brighton Municipal Constabulary?" then continued without waiting for an answer, "Because he knows of you all right. Proper pissed off with you, he is." Fisher placed one of the telegrams face down on the desk and began reading the next. Wheatley did what every policeman learned to do when receiving a dressing down from a superior — stood to attention, gazed at the wall and remained silent.

"Oh no, we don't do the silent resignation 'yes sir', 'no sir', act here, matey. Not when we are here disobeying orders. Not when we are trespassing without a by-your-leave on the manor of another Force. Not when we try to interrogate on said manor, not only a peer of the realm but a magistrate I have to deal with every bloody day. And worse of all, whose wife bends my ear on the telephone about her husband and allegations of dirty weekends and nieces in Brighton of all places."

The Inspector had removed his feet from the desk and sat for a few moments concentrating on the sheaf of telegrams, throwing them on the desk in front of him before looking up and saying, "Well? And look at me when I'm talking to you, constable."

Wheatley was at a loss. Seeing his career disappearing before his eyes, all he could think of to say was, "Sorry."

"Sorry. He says sorry." Inspector Fisher's look was more of resignation than anger. "Sit!" he said, pointing to a chair in front of the desk, its seat piled with more files. "And we say 'Sorry, sir,' around here when speaking to a superior officer."

"Sorry, sir," said Wheatley meekly, before removing the pile of files to the floor and sinking gratefully onto the chair.

"OK, son," said the Inspector, "tell me all about it."

It took a long time. Inspector Fisher was a patient and skilled interrogator. Wheatley was unsure why the Inspector needed such detail, but he was so depressed about the failure of his mission and the effect that might have on his future career that he co-operated without question. At last Inspector Fisher seemed to be satisfied. He picked up the sheaf of telegrams on his desk, sorted through until he found the one he was looking for, and proceeded to read it. Wheatley wondered if this was his dismissal. Should he stand up and leave? He was examining this dilemma, shifting slightly in his chair as he decided to make a run for it, sinking into stillness as he decided to sit it out when the Inspector shouted

"Simmonds," before replacing the telegram back on the pile in front of him and looking expectantly at the door. Almost immediately the smaller of the two detectives who had accosted Wheatley opened the door and peered quizzically into the office, saying "Guv'nor?"

"Tell the Professor to get in here," said the Inspector before turning to Wheatley and saying, "Sounds right up his street, this one." Wheatley waited for more information as to how a case in Brighton could be 'right up the street' of a professor but Inspector Fisher just kept his own counsel, clasping his hands in front of him and humming quietly. Wheatley decided the wisest thing was to remain still and silent.

Simmonds had left the door open and soon there was a quiet knock and a man entered the room. As he approached the desk, Inspector Fisher said to Wheatley, "This here is Detective Constable Jerome Winstanley, otherwise known as 'the Professor', or 'Prof' for short, because unlike the rest of us ignoramuses he actually went to school."

In front of Wheatley stood the most unlikely looking police constable he had ever seen. He was a small man, almost delicate looking, probably in his early thirties but already balding. He was wearing a smart suit, highly polished shoes and spats of all things. A black ribbon around his neck supported his pince-nez, which he removed to peer at Wheatley as the Inspector continued, "And this here is…" nodding towards Wheatley and raising his eyebrows.

"Just Wheatley. Call me Wheatley, everyone does," said Wheatley.

"How do you do?" said Detective Winstanley before turning to Inspector Fisher, saying, "Was it just for introductions I was summoned or did you want me for anything else, guv?" Winstanley formed his words very precisely and Wheatley found the strange term 'Guv' at odds with his plummy accent.

"Sit down, Prof, and stop being so bleeding insubordinate," said Inspector Fisher before turning to Wheatley and saying, "Detective Winstanley is our resident shysters, tricksters and con-men expert as well as our interpreter of the upper classes. I think he might find your story familiar."

"I see," said Wheatley, while thinking that he didn't see at all.

"Well?" said the inspector when the men had been sitting in silence for half a minute or so.

"Sir?" said Wheatley as he realised Inspector Fisher was addressing him.

"Tell the bloody story."

"But I've already…"

"Yes, but the prof wasn't here then, was he? He's clever but he ain't clairvoyant."

Wheatley told his story again. This time the Inspector kept quiet, but Detective Winstanley quizzed Wheatley in detail about Sir Toby's appearance and seemed particularly interested that he had shaken hands in greeting. When Wheatley had finished and sat back, exhausted by over two hours of questioning, the two London detectives looked at each other.

"Slimy Cecil?" said Inspector Fisher.

"Sounds like him," confirmed Detective Winstanley.

"Who's Slimy Cecil?" asked Wheatley.

"Cecil deVere he calls himself, in reality Charlie Runcorn, a superior type of confidence trickster what we've been trying to put away, unsuccessfully I might add, for more years than I care to remember. Winstanley here will fill you in on the way to Brighton."

"On the way to Brighton?" said Wheatley, who was rather confused by the way the conversation was going. "Is Detective Winstanley to escort me?"

"Accompany, not escort," said the Inspector, "You'll need him for identification."

"Identification?"

"Of the body." As he said this, the Inspector picked up the telegram he had been perusing earlier and held it out to Wheatley. "You've got another corpse, and from the description, it's Slimy Cecil; your Sir Toby Hughes-Lewthwaite and our Charlie Runcorn."

*

The journey from London had passed quickly, a cab from Savile Row to Victoria and an express train to Brighton had them walking towards the Town Hall in less than two hours. Despite Inspector Fisher's comment that Detective Winstanley would 'fill in the details' for Wheatley on the journey, their train conversation had consisted mainly of Winstanley lamenting that cricket was not played in winter and then quizzing Wheatley about Sussex County Cricket Club. Wheatley knew that the cricket ground was near his digs but apart from that had little knowledge of the game. This mattered not a jot. Winstanley kept up a constant stream of cricketing anecdotes even during the walk from the station until, passing through the market square he ceased mid-sentence.

"What is that infernal racket?"

"Racket," said Wheatley. "What racket?"

"That," said Winstanley. "That terrible screeching."

"Do you mean the gulls?" asked Wheatley, observing the common sight of herring gulls fighting over the detritus remaining after the daily market. "They're just birds."

"Birds?" said Winstanley, "Banshees more like. I thought the pigeons back home were bad enough, but those monsters…"

"We're here," said Wheatley indicating the Town Hall.

As they entered the Police Station, Wheatley could feel his heart beating faster. And not for no reason. As soon as they passed through the door, Sergeant Johnson jerked alert and called "The Inspector wants to see you, Wheatley. As soon as you came in, he said." Then, returning to his ledgers, he added, "Wouldn't want to be you, lad, proper paddy he was in," all the time shaking his head sorrowfully.

"Better go and face the music, I suppose," Wheatley said to Winstanley, "I'll show you where you can wait."

"Not at all, old boy, I'll come with you," said Winstanley, adding, "if you don't mind, of course. I need a word with your inspector chappie. This way, is it?"

Once in the office, Wheatley was surprised to see the Inspector was not in his usual position by the fire but in front of his pristine desk, leaning backwards against it. As he saw Wheatley, he pushed himself upright and drew breath, but any indignant speech was prevented by Detective Winstanley striding forwards.

"Winstanley, Metropolitan Police, Marylebone. So pleased to meet you, Inspector Cronin." Taken unawares, Inspector Cronin's good manners surfaced and as Winstanley had his right hand stretched out, the two men shook hands. As soon as they did this, Wheatley noticed a change in the Inspector's demeanour — he was almost beaming! It was true that Winstanley's already superior accent had raised itself yet another notch but surely something else had affected the Inspector who was now saying, "Pleased to meet you, too, Inspector Winstanley."

"Alas, no," said Winstanley, "merely a Detective Constable."

"Really?" said Cronin, "Amazing. I took you for an Oxford man."

"Cambridge, actually," said Winstanley. "Now sorry to get to business so quickly but I really must convey the Metropolitan Police Force's thanks for Detective Wheatley."

"Yes, Wheatley," said the Inspector scowling towards the bemused Detective, then, doing a double take, turned back to Winstanley and said, "Thanks?"

"Yes, a master stroke by your good self to send him into our neck of the woods, if I may say so, Inspector. We believe that the person he is investigating is a master criminal we have been trying to apprehend for ages. I am here to confirm that very fact as soon as we have to, regrettably, leave your company."

"Master criminal?" said the Inspector.

"Yes, and thanks to Detective Constable Wheatley, we can write a myriad of crimes from our books. My inspector, Inspector Fisher, sends his compliments and his thanks. Indeed, he has an interview with the Commissioner today to comment on the extraordinary co-operation by the Brighton Constabulary. Wouldn't be surprised if there wasn't a commendation in it for you."

"Commendation?"

"And justly deserved, I'm sure," said Winstanley. "Now, if there's nothing else, sir, my young friend and I must press on. I need to identify the miscreant and get back to London this evening."

"Well…" said Inspector Cronin, who had shifted his gaze towards Wheatley.

"You know, I'm sure we've met before," said Winstanley, returning the Inspector's attention back to himself, "perhaps in our Varsity days?"

"Yes, now you come to mention it, there is something familiar about you," said Cronin.

"Possibly at Henley? I coxed the eight in '80 and '81."

"Didn't row." The Inspector looked a little crestfallen at this, but rallied with, "Fencing was my forte at Oxford."

"A fellow blue, I knew it," said Winstanley, seizing the Inspector's hand and shaking it vigorously. "So good to meet you, old chap." And with that he turned and bustled Wheatley from the office.

"What happened in there?" asked Wheatley as they descended the stairs back towards the detective office.

"Tell you later," said Winstanley, "but I don't think you'll have any more trouble from him about your little trip. Now, shall we get on with the identification?"

"But even so, a commendation. From the Commissioner," said Wheatley.

"Don't be naïve, Wheatley," scorned Winstanley. "If Inspector Fisher ever gets to see the Commissioner it will be to be hauled over the carpet. I just said all that to get you off the hook."

"But..." said Wheatley as Winstanley disappeared down the stairs muttering, "Master criminal. Commendation indeed. Pompous ass! And fencing was just a half-blue in my day." Wheatley shrugged and went to organise a runner to inform Shadrach Mears that they were on their way to view the body.

*

Shadrach was not happy. This visit there was no theatrical revealing of the deceased, no hymn singing, no clean collar and tie. Indeed, Shadrach Mears seemed to have made himself as unkempt as possible, his brown porter's coat covered by an extremely grubby blood-stained apron. Instead of the modern 'necroscopy facility', he had escorted the two detectives into the dank cellar-like interior of the mortuary and the cadaver was viewed by the light of a hand-held oil lantern. It took Winstanley only a minute or two to confirm that the corpse was indeed that of Charles Runcorn, also known as Cecil deVere, Slimy Cecil, and to Wheatley, Sir Tobias Hughes-Lewthwaite, baronet.

"Now can we get out of here?" he said to Wheatley. "I'll fill you in on the way to the station."

As they left, Shadrach grudgingly passed an envelope to Wheatley which turned out to be a request from Dr Buchanan that he attend her at her 'office' at five pm on the following Monday to get the results of the necroscopy.

"Why do I have to wait until Monday?" he complained.

"Cos it's the weekend," said Mears. "Dr Buchanan don't work weekends, goes to the country or something."

"Though she never says which country," he added.

"But this is urgent, it's a murder investigation," said Wheatley.

"She'll do the necroscopy on Monday. You can have the results after that. Unless, of course, you want to watch, which will cost you five bob for yours truly," he continued, before closing the door firmly in the face of the two detectives.

*

"Charlie Runcorn was a clever, annoyingly clever, type of confidence trickster," said Detective Winstanley.

Wheatley and Winstanley were sitting in a quiet area of the bar of the Railway Hotel opposite Brighton Station. Winstanley had apologised for not telling all he knew before about 'Slimy Cecil', but said he needed to be sure that they had the right man first. He suggested they went for a drink on the way to catch his train when he would tell all. Wheatley rarely frequented public houses. Although his parents had imbibed, he had never got the taste for it. He found the beer which Detective Edwards consumed so enthusiastically bitter and unappetising. He had enjoyed the brandy Dr Buchanan had 'prescribed' for him, particularly its warming sensations, but in the end, he settled for a half pint of shandy-gaff when Winstanley asked "What'll you have?", the sweetness of the ginger beer mitigating somewhat the bitterness of the ale. Detective Winstanley had also ordered a single and a double malt whisky, downed the single at the bar, then carried the double to the table.

"Charlie is, or now I suppose, was, drawn to the haunts of the rich," Winstanley continued once they were settled in a quiet corner of the public house. "He's been identified all over the country: Tunbridge Wells, Harrogate, Leamington Spa, Bath. Should have thought of Brighton, just his type of place in the Season. We even suspect he's been operating abroad. Certainly a report last year from Paris about an English 'Milord' leaving Le Touquet with reams of debts seems to fit his modus operandi."

The detective paused to sip his drink as Wheatley asked, "You don't have London on that list, so why is it you investigating?"

"Marylebone Police District has the misfortune to house many of the aristocracy like Sir Tobias Hughes-Lewthwaite. Using his alias Cecil deVere, Charlie collects information about them, where they live, who they know, that sort of thing, then goes off to some watering hole for the season assuming their identity. He runs up massive debts, living the high life and borrowing large sums from the local big knobs he meets at the nearest lodge."

"Lodge?" said Wheatley.

"Masonic Lodge," said Winstanley, then, when Wheatley looked at him uncomprehendingly added, "You are aware of the organisation known as the Freemasons?"

"There's a Freemason's Hall on Western Road," said Wheatley. "Decorated with strange symbols, but I always assumed it was some type of religion."

Winstanley chuckled at that. "I suppose in a way you're right," he said. "Look, you asked me how I was able to mollify your Inspector Cronin."

"Yes, I meant to thank you for that," but Winstanley was already holding his right hand out towards him saying, "Shake my hand." Wheatley wondered where all this was leading but did so, using the strong, manly grip he had practiced on the hand towel in the bedroom of his digs. Winstanley, though, swivelled his hand and Wheatley felt a thumb press twice on the space between the joints of his index finger. "What was that?" he asked.

"The Freemasons are a semi-secret international order for men only which they will say descends from the Knights Templar and Knights of St John and dedicated to doing good. In fact, it is a society for advantaging and enriching its members. Most of the male members of the Royal Family are said to be Masons and the great and the good fall over themselves to follow suit. They have secret handshakes among other things to identify themselves to one another. I've just shown you one of them."

"So that's why Sir Toby's handshake was so peculiar when I met him. He was a Mason."

"Not exactly," said Winstanley. "He never was a pukka Lodge member as far as I can tell, but he knew all the rituals at least well enough to pass muster for a short time. Same again?"

Wheatley's head was streaming with questions, so he hardly noticed the London detective visit the bar and return with another round of drinks. "Drink up," he said, nodding at Wheatley's three-quarters-full glass and putting a fresh one next to it. Wheatley noticed that Winstanley's speech had gone decidedly down register since he had launched into his explanation of 'Slimy Cecil's' peccadillos.

"So, Charlie, pretending to be 'Lord So-and-so' will descend on a fashionable resort accompanied by an attractive female accomplice, usually some upper-quality brass he's picked up. He obtains accommodation on credit, arranges accounts at various establishments while looking for an appropriate person to use his dodgy handshake on. Then introductions, and an invite to the local Lodge. Once he's in with the locals, he begs, borrows and steals until the end of the season when he disappears. When the real 'Lord So-and-so' starts getting polite, and less polite, requests for repayment of loans, final demands and summonses, he kicks up a fuss and it all lands on my desk. I tell you Wheatley, Charlie Runcorn lying dead in your mortuary will clear up several boxes of unsolved cases for us. Inspector Fisher will be very relieved to get the local gentry off his back." Winstanley settled back and pulled a pocket watch from his waistcoat, opening its face and saying, "Nearly time for my train," before draining his glass and preparing to leave.

"Wait," said Wheatley, desperate to prevent the detective leaving before he had gained as much information as he could.

"Wait, why? What for? I've told you all you need to know."

"The girl," said Wheatley, "why involve a girl?"

"Well," said Detective Winstanley, "women aren't allowed in a Masonic Lodge of course, but when meeting acquaintances for social occasions, you can get away with anything using the distraction of an attractive woman flashing her eyes at your victim."

"Or her other attributes," he continued. "Now I must go."

Wheatley had so many questions he was getting desperate. "The drinks," he squeaked.

"The drinks?"

Wheatley returned his voice to its usual timbre.

"After all, you've bought me two drinks. Hospitality demands that I buy you one. And you haven't explained about Inspector Cronin yet."

Winstanley had risen to his feet, but he paused, seemed to think deeply, then bumped back down in his seat saying, "That's awfully civil, old fellow, don't mind if I do. There will be another train along soon, I'm sure."

Accent's going up register again, thought Wheatley as he fetched the drinks, another double malt for Winstanley, and this time a small brandy for himself.

"Yes, the Inspector Cronin," said Winstanley. "I guessed he was a Freemason when you told me about him defending Sir Toby and saying things like he was 'on the level' and 'straight as a die.' Masonic terms you see. And once I used the secret handshake… You see how it works?"

"So you are a Mason too?"

"Once, long ago. But not practicing now. Us brave boys in blue shouldn't be serving two masters. Will eventually lead to conflict, you see."

"But why the murder? And why did Sir Toby, er, Charlie, stay on after the Season? And why did his so-called niece disappear? Where is she?"

"All conundrii, dear boy, and I am glad to say, on your desk, not mine."

Wheatley hadn't touched his brandy, but Detective Winstanley had finished his Scotch and struggled unsteadily to his feet.

"Mind you, I shouldn't be surprised if old Charlie had rooked the wrong person and got his comeuppance. Good riddance, I say. Farewell, young man, good hunting."

With this final comment, he moved unsteadily through the door, leaving Wheatley to consider Detective Winstanley's sliding accent and wonder if Charlie Runcorn was the only con-artist.

Saturday 10th February 1894

TAP, TAP, TAP on the window. Then again: TAP, TAP, TAP. Wheatley jerked awake at the sound of the lamplighter 'knocking up' the sleeping residents of the street, letting them know it was time for work. He immediately regretted the sudden movement as a bolt of pain flashed through his head. He remembered that he was not on duty today. He and Edwards shared duty at the weekends, meaning each of them got a Saturday or Sunday off. *A bit like when I was young*, he had thought when this had been explained to him. Saturday as the rest day when his Jewish mother held sway in the house, Sunday, when his Catholic father was dominant. But today was Saturday and Wheatley's day off this week. Which he was grateful for because he was certainly unwell. His head pounded, his stomach was decidedly queasy and his mouth felt dry and foetid. Reaching for the glass of water on his bedside table, Wheatley realised that instead of his usual nightshirt, he seemed to be fully dressed. He pulled himself upright, which was a mistake. His stomach performed a somersault, his head pounded, and he took a moment to collect himself. Slowly he moved to open his curtains. It was more than an hour before dawn but there was sufficient light for him to survey his room. He was pleased to see its familiar orderly self. His washstand in front of the window still contained his shaving things: razor, shaving mug and brush neatly laid out, soap and flannel next to them, his strop hanging from the side. A side table to the right of the window held a mirror on a swivel stand, a folded towel and his hairbrush and comb. The tallboy opposite the brass single bed was exactly as he had left it, drawers and doors firmly closed. On the hook behind the door, though, was an empty hanger. A hanger which usually held his night-shirt during the day and his suit while he slept. His suit, the trousers and waistcoat of which he seemed to be already wearing. Turning back towards the bed, the mystery deepened. Hanging from the brass balls decorating the bedstead at the foot of the bed were his jacket on one side, his night shirt on the other and on the floor between them were his boots. The bed itself was ruffled but fully made up, the sheets and blankets firmly tucked in. He appeared to have slept on top of the covers with just the bedspread over him. Wheatley regarded all of this in confusion, trying to think what could have caused such a lapse. He remembered the Station Hotel and his conversation with Detective Winstanley clearly. He remembered drinking his brandy as Winstanley left to get his train, and drinking another, a large one this time, while he tried to make sense of the case. After that things seemed to get hazy. He knew he had taken the train rather than his usual omnibus — it made sense being so close to the station. And he might have had another drink in the station buffet whilst waiting for the train. But after he got off at

Hove, he was certain he had walked straight home. Or did he? Something about the Eclipse Inn on the corner of Montgomery Street was surfacing at the back of his mind.

Wheatley sat down on the bed and put his head in his hands, realising that far from the bout of influenza he had imagined when he woke up feeling so awful, he had what was known as 'bottle-ache', graphically described to him by Detective Edwards and other colleagues but never before experienced. He stood up again — too quickly — sank back on the bed, placed his hands under his thighs, swivelled to take in his whole domain once more, stood and walked to the mirror, rubbed his hands roughly through his hair and finally stilled, gazing unfocusedly through his window, willing the nausea to settle. When he felt he had gained some control of himself, he crossed to the bedroom door and opened it to retrieve the jug of hot water left there for him every morning. Washing and shaving, changing into a clean shirt and collar calmed Wheatley somewhat. Although he still felt what he would definitely describe as 'fragile', he resolved to face the world and headed downstairs to the communal dining room of his lodging house.

When he had been a constable with the Brunswick Town Watch, Wheatley had had accommodation provided for him in Brunswick Square so that he had only to step from the front door of his boarding house to be at work. His move to the Brighton Municipal Constabulary had necessitated a change of lodgings and he had thought himself fortunate to have obtained a room at Mrs Harris's

Home for Temperate Gentlemen. For just under two-thirds of his pay, he got a comfortable room to himself, two square meals a day, hot water every morning for washing and shaving and one small bag of laundry washed and ironed every fortnight. This was facilitated by the formidable Mrs Harris, who did all the supervising, and her companion, Mrs Lee, who did all the work. True, these lodgings were rather a long way from his place of employment, being on the extreme western edge of Hove at the corner of Clarendon Villas Road and Westbourne Street. But having been built within the last few years, the house had all modern advantages, including gaslight in every room and even an internal water closet. Since securing this accommodation, Wheatley had become used to the journey, often walking home to clear his mind from a difficult day. His room was on the first floor along with four others, while two more occupied the attic space. All were rented by gentlemen he would nod to at meals but rarely had any meaningful conversation with.

As Wheatley descended the stairs, he hoped that this day he would be alone in the dining room. Breakfast was a casual affair with the affable Mrs Lee happy to serve the gentlemen as they arrived. The formal evening meal, however, was a different matter. Presided over by Mrs Harris, she expected everyone to arrive on time and be ready in the dining room when she left her ground floor apartment at seven pm sharp to take her place at the head of the table.

Today he was fortunate. The table showed signs of several of the lodgers having breakfasted before him, but the room was blessedly empty. Wheatley helped himself to a strong cup of tea from the pot on the sideboard, studiously ignored the hotplate sitting next to it, and sat at the table to sip the scalding liquid. His time alone was brief. Firstly Mrs Lee ascended from the kitchen in the basement with a tray in her hand ready to clear the table.

"Oh, Mr Wheatley, it's nice to see you back on your feet, we were so worried about you last night."

Wheatley stared horrified at Mrs Lee wondering what he couldn't remember about the previous evening. Had he disgraced himself? Were apologies required? Fortunately, Mrs Lee busied herself piling the tray with dirty crockery and did not seem too put out when she continued, "It's fried eggs this morning, Mr Wheatley, and I've cooked up some lovely kidneys in the hotplate to go with them."

Wheatley's stomach turned over at the thought.

"Just some dry toast this morning, please, Mrs Lee."

"Still not quite right, eh?" Mrs Lee said sympathetically before disappearing through the door towards the kitchen.

Sitting with another cup of tea and willing himself to recover, Wheatley was again interrupted as a guest he recognised as one of the attic residents entered the room and gave a cheery 'Good Morning'. He proceeded to serve himself a cup of tea before sitting down opposite Wheatley. Wheatley nodded in greeting, remembering to move his head slowly, as Mrs Lee returned.

"Here's your toast, Mr Wheatley," she said, then, "Fried eggs today, Mr Pettit, I'm sure *you* will have some."

"Ambrosia, Mrs Lee. Of course, I'll have your delicious eggs."

"And there's some nice kidneys to go with them on the hotplate."

Mr Pettit held a grin until she had left the room, then exhaled.

"Dear God, what is it with those women and offal? Tripe and onions last night for supper, Wheatley, you were lucky to miss it." Wheatley felt his stomach lurch but managed to maintain his equilibrium. Pettit said, "Sorry, what was I thinking? Last thing you want to think about after last night, I'm sure. How are you feeling by the way?"

"Fine, thank you," lied Wheatley

"Hair of the dog, old chap, hair of the dog. Only cure."

Wheatley sat mortified. This man, who he barely knew, seemed to know all about last night. A lot more than Wheatley did himself, anyway. Breathing in slowly through his nose, Wheatley steeled himself to ask the questions he was dreading.

"Truth is, Pettit, last night seems a little hazy. Did I make a complete ass of myself?"

"Not at all, not at all, As far as anyone in the house is concerned you were ill and had taken to your bed."

"How did that come about?" asked Wheatley, who was experiencing a little hope deep down inside. Either that or his stomach was complaining about the morsel of dry toast he had just swallowed.

"Ah, well... Imagine the scene, Wheatley. Six of us standing behind our chairs hungry for supper. The clock strikes seven. In walks Mrs Harris to stand at the head of the table. We wait for her to sit. She doesn't. 'Where is Mr Wheatley?' she asks. 'Not like him to be late.' 'Perhaps he's working late again,' says that Mr Davidson from the room at the back."

Wheatley who had been slumped in his chair disconsolately, perked up at this. "It's true, I'm often out for supper," he said, but was ignored by Mr Pettit who ploughed on with his story.

" 'Nonsense,' says Mrs Harris, 'I heard him climbing the stairs and entering his room a scant half-hour ago'."

At this Wheatley slumped even further, his head in his hands, all hope of salvaging his reputation gone. This time Pettit did cease his tale.

"Heard, Wheatley, not saw," he said, seeming to intuit Wheatley's fears. "I'll put you out of your misery, old chap. I volunteered to pop up and get you, saw the situation and returned to tell the others that you were feeling poorly and had taken an early night. Mrs Harris sat down. We all sat down. Mrs Lee brought in the tripe.

"And good wholesome food it was," he said loudly as Mrs Lee entered with his plate of eggs.

"Glad you liked it, Mr Pettit. Excuse me, but I couldn't help overhearing about the tripe," said Mrs Lee placing the eggs down in front of him and warning him that the plate was hot before saying, "so you'll be pleased to know it is liver and bacon for supper tonight," as she left the room.

"At least there's bacon," said Pettit, checking that they were truly alone before saying to Wheatley, "As far as everyone is concerned, you were taken ill last night and your reputation is unblemished."

Wheatley was alternately relieved he had not made a fool of himself, concerned that Pettit had witnessed his disgrace and confused about the sequence of events. He supposed he owed his fellow resident thanks but needed now to know the awful truth. All of it.

"What did you mean when you said you 'saw the situation'?" he asked.

"Are you sure you want all the gory details?" said Pettit, "Isn't it better to let sleeping dogs lie?"

"All the details," confirmed Wheatley.

"Very well," said Pettit.

He didn't begin immediately. Wheatley had to wait while Pettit ate his breakfast 'before it gets cold,' and poured another cup of tea. But eventually he settled back and told of how he had gone to Wheatley's door, entering the room when his knock received no answer. "The gas was lit," he said, "your nightshirt, jacket and the bedspread were crumpled up on the floor and you were flat out on the bed, snoring."

"Why didn't you just wake me?" asked Wheatley, ignoring the rudeness of the snoring remark.

Wheatley noticed Pettit looking at him intently as if trying to make up his mind about something before continuing. "I had to make a decision about what to do. I suppose I could have woken you but well, quite frankly, old chap, you stank of spirits. This *is* officially a Temperance house and you know what a tartar Mrs H is. So, I hung up your nightshirt and jacket, removed your footwear, loosened your collar and tucked you in using the bedspread. All without you waking I might add. Then I turned out the gas and went back downstairs to tell a little white lie."

Wheatley stared at the man opposite who was smiling back at him. He knew little about Pettit, just gossip one picked up here and there. He had always considered him a bit of a dilletante and even now noted he was sitting down to breakfast in a soft-collared shirt, no jacket and wearing bedroom slippers! But even so Wheatley owed him thanks for saving his reputation, and knowing Mrs Harris' views on the demon drink, for keeping a roof over his head.

"I owe you my thanks," said Wheatley formally, standing and holding out his hand.

"Think nothing of it, old chap," said Pettit, standing and shaking Wheatley's hand properly and certainly not in a secret way before walking to the sideboard.

"Another cup that cheers but not inebriates?"

It was pleasant sitting and sharing a cup of tea with an affable companion. Wheatley was enjoying himself despite still feeling delicate. Today he could sit for as long as he wished and certainly Mr Pettit seemed in no hurry. But as always, the case was turning over at the back of Wheatley's mind and there was also something about

Pettit that was nagging him. Slowly he brought it back into his consciousness. He had recognised Pettit before. In Brighton, not in the boarding house. On the seafront.

"You're an artist of some sort, aren't you?" he said.

"Of some sort, yes," said Pettit, smirking.

"I remember seeing you sometime last summer. By the West Pier, sketching tourists."

"That's how I make my crust in the summer. Sometimes I get the odd commission, a real portrait, but usually it's just quick sketches for the tourists."

"And in the winter?" asked Wheatley.

"With what I make in the Season and the odd commercial work, signwriting, advertisements, that sort of thing, I can sometimes eke my way through the winter," said Pettit. "Otherwise, it's the dogs."

"The dogs?" Wheatley wondered whether this was a new term for poverty that he hadn't heard before.

"Yes, dogs. When desperate, I haunt the gardens and squares of Hove seafront looking for old ladies out walking their dogs. You know the sort, all doting and treating their pets like lovers. 'Precious' this and 'Sweetums' that. Even let the curs lick their faces."

Wheatley could see disgust on Pettit's face. "And then?" he asked.

"Then I make a fuss of their darlings, spin a sad story about a faithful old hound I lost recently to that great bone-yard in the sky, and drop into the conversation that I'm an animal artist."

"You had a dog? Here?"

103

"Obviously not. Can you imagine Mrs H's face? It's just a story to get a commission."

"And that works?"

"Usually about once a week. Every now and then I persuade the owner to have a portrait with their pet. For double the fee, of course. But usually it's just pencil sketches of dogs."

Pettit lapsed into silence, gazing into his empty teacup.

"But you are a proper portrait artist really?" Wheatley clarified.

"I don't know about proper," said Pettit, "but a portrait artist certainly. Why, would you like a sketch? Or even a portrait of yourself? I could give you a good price."

Wheatley ignored the suddenly enthusiastic artist. His mind was racing. He had a photograph of the dead woman found on the beach. A photograph taken after the autopsy certainly, but a sufficient likeness all the same. What he didn't have was a likeness of the missing 'Miss Stephanie'.

"Could you make a sketch of someone's face if it was described to you?"

Pettit frowned. "Certainly, but it would take some time. Why do you ask?"

*

"Good afternoon, Edwards," said Wheatley, carefully entering the Detective Office.

"Isn't it your day off, Wheatley? I mean, keen is keen, but…"

"Believe me, I would be home nursing my head if it wasn't so urgent."

Wheatley shared the discomfort of his nagging headache and churning stomach with Detective Edwards. It had been ameliorated a little by the sea air as Wheatley had walked into Brighton, but not cured. Edwards tutted in sympathy, left the room and returned with a glass of water and a box labelled *'Emerson's Bromo Selzer; All headaches instantly cured or your money back'*. He removed a teaspoon from his pocket, measured three spoonsful into the water glass and stirred the liquid until it began to foam.

"Here, drink this. All down in one go, mind. Soon have you right as rain."

Wheatley drank the fizzing liquid before carefully placing the empty glass on the desk in front of him and saying, "Well if anything will get me to forget my headache, the taste of that will," and shuddered. "Where did you get it from so quickly?"

"Sergeant Johnson always has a box behind the counter. Comes in handy to pep up any of the boys who arrive on duty having had a hard night, if you see what I mean. Now tell me about this idea that won't wait."

"It was just a stroke of luck really," said Wheatley. He went on to explain to Detective Edwards his idea about using Millie to describe the missing woman to Pettit who would produce a likeness.

"I sent a telegram to Millie asking her to meet us here and Mr Pettit will be arriving shortly," he finished.

"Can't hurt, I suppose. Very nice of this artist fella to do it for free," said Edwards. Then, staring intently at Wheatley, said, "he *is* doing it for free isn't he?"

"Sort of," said Wheatley.

Seeing Edwards' face change, he said hastily, "Don't worry, I explained that there couldn't be a fee this time."

"This time?"

"Well, I might have said that if he became a well-known police artist, he could get some lucrative commissions."

"Police artist," snorted Edwards. "No such thing."

"Well, perhaps there should be," said Wheatley.

At that moment, Sergeant Johnson poked his head around the door and said, "Visitor for you, Wheatley," before propelling Mr Pettit into the office and departing, muttering about having better things to do than escort civilians about the place. There was only enough time to placate the artist and for introductions before the door opened again and Millie entered the room, saying over her shoulder, "Thank you so much, Sergeant Johnson."

Wheatley's jaw dropped and he looked at Detective Edwards and Mr Pettit in amazement as they heard Sergeant Johnson saying, "Think nothing of it, miss, a real pleasure."

"What a lovely man that sergeant is." said Millie. Then after a moment of silence, she said, "Right, shall we get started?"

The artist was the first to recover, saying, "Where shall I set up, Mr Wheatley?"

"Well, here," said Wheatley.

"No, this won't do at all, no natural light, you see."

"There's a small window in the parading hall," offered Edwards.

"No," said Pettit, "I need the studio to be flooded with light, preferably from a south-facing window."

"Well, the only place like that is the inspector's office, and he wouldn't agree to anyone using it, even though he's never here at weekends," said Wheatley.

"Knocks off early on Fridays, too," said Edwards. "He waited here specially yesterday Wheatley to give you a bollocking. What happened about that anyway?"

"I'll tell you later," said Wheatley.

Edwards nodded, then continued, "Pity he locks his office door when he's not there. He'd never know if we used it and the room *is* standing empty."

"Does his own cleaning, do he?" said Millie.

"What do you mean, Millie?" asked Edwards.

"Well, someone must have a key," she said. "Unless the cleaner gets in through the keyhole."

Wheatley looked at Edwards and they both said in unison, "Sergeant Johnson!"

"Well, that's that. Hell will freeze over before Sergeant Johnson risks his pension by doing a favour for the likes of us," said Edwards.

Wheatley was seeing his plan unravelling when Mr Pettit asked, "Where has the young lady gone?" The door was open, and Millie had seemingly slipped out.

"I'll go and see if I can find her," sighed Wheatley, but before he could move, Millie returned, triumphantly holding up a ring of keys.

"That nice Sergeant Johnson says it's the smallest key, the others open the cells or something," said Millie. "And he says don't leave no trace in there or he'll have your guts for garters."

Sunday 11th February 1894

Wheatley sat at the desk in the detective office and carefully unfolded the pencil sketch of the missing 'Miss Stephanie' which Millie had assured him was an excellent likeness. Yesterday, Mr Pettit and Millie had returned to Wheatley and Edwards after about an hour and a half entrenched in the Inspector's office.

"Don't worry, there's nothing out of place," Millie assured Wheatley. "See you next Wednesday, don't forget," she went on before adding, "unless there's anything you want to see me for before then, of course. Anything at all." Then she left to return the office key to 'that nice Sergeant Johnson', and make her way home.

"What a stunner," Pettit had said.

"Not so sure about that," said Detective Edwards regarding the sketch "Bit of a disappointment. Eyes too small. And too close together."

"I wasn't talking about the sketch," said Pettit, "I was talking about Miss Millie Stephens. You're a lucky dog, Wheatley."

Now, sitting regarding the sketch on this quiet Sunday morning, Wheatley had to admit that Miss Stephanie was not quite the beauty she had been made out to be. *I suppose beauty is in the eyes of the beholder*, he thought to himself.

His mind drifted to Millie's eyes, which were far superior to the pictured lady's. More lustrous, almost liquid…

Wheatley shook his head to pull himself out of such thoughts. After all, he assured himself, he had always acted with the utmost decorum towards Millie. He didn't think of her in that way. Though he wasn't at all sure what 'that way' was. It was others who had made assumptions about a relationship that didn't exist. Was that the way Millie saw it? She certainly seemed to be making assumptions of her own. Wheatley felt completely out of his depth and so did what he always did when floundering emotionally — immersed himself in work. Deciding he needed some air, he set out to see the only pawnbroker yet to be visited by the constables trying to find the effects of the missing woman.

*

"Mr Policeman Wheatley, what can I do for you today?"

The old man was sat behind his fortified counter wearing an ancient fedora and a heavy overcoat and wrapped tightly in his tallit looking exactly as he had five days ago when Wheatley had visited in preparation for a raid to recover stolen property. True, the shelves and cubby-holes behind the counter were less crowded, but otherwise the shop contained the familiar hodgepodge of clothes racks, trunks, packing cases and umbrella stands.

"Mr Zimmerman, I'm a little surprised to see you here," said Wheatley. "I only came on the off chance."

"Always open on Sundays. I close on Saturdays, my Sabbath."

"After our last encounter, I'm surprised to see the shop open, surprised to see you at liberty."

Mr Zimmerman nodded, rocking on his stool slightly but maintained his silence.

"And," Wheatley added, "even more surprised now you know who I am that you let me in." He remembered the pawnbroker's entry system which was operated from behind the counter.

"Mr Wheatley," said the old man, pulling his shawl closer around himself, "I never turn away a good customer. As for that other thing, a mere misunderstanding."

"A misunderstanding? With over a hundred pounds worth of stolen goods recovered from your shop?"

Mr Zimmerman shrugged and raised his hands. "Such a way to treat the kindness of an old man. I give my nephew employment and that is how he repays me. Stolen goods. In *my* shop. I should never have taken him on. That mother of his! But what can you do when it's family?" Sadly, he raised his hands and covered his eyes.

"But you were both indicted, I saw the papers," said Wheatley.

"Fortunately the magistrate, a great judge of character, a King Solomon of a man, realised how the young scoundrel had duped his poor confused old uncle," said Mr Zimmerman, dropping his hands to below the counter. "So, he incarcerated my nephew deservedly in Lewes Prison to await trial. But as for me, sent me home cleared of all blame. He even sent his clerk with me to ensure I got home safely in my addled state. Wonderful man."

The two men remained in silence for a minute or two ruminating on their varied opinions of said magistrate. Eventually Mr Zimmerman stirred and asked again what he could do for the young detective.

"I couldn't help noticing as I passed the window a lady's hat, the one with an ostrich feather. I think it might pertain to a case of mine."

"You have good taste, Mr Policeman Wheatley, such good taste," the old man said, wincing as he got down from his stool and opened the door which barred the way to the counter and the storeroom beyond. Wheatley couldn't help noticing that the door opened easily with a faint click, unlike the key fumbling routine necessary to open it when Sergeant Johnson was raging to get behind the counter and into the storeroom during the raid.

A padlocked metal grid prevented access to the windows from inside the shop while still allowing light through. Mr Zimmerman opened the padlock, reached into the window to take out the hat Wheatley had described, relocked the grid and made his way slowly back to his stool, making sure that the access door was firmly closed behind him.

"This hat?" he said.

"It looks like one we've been searching for. Did you see who brought it in?"

"Yes, a young lady. Most attractive. Sold a few other bits and pieces."

"Did you get a name and address?"

"No, sorry, Mr Policeman. She sold, not pledged. So no reason for an address."

Wheatley had supposed such to be so but was hopeful that at least his pictures would establish identity. "Was this the girl?" he said laying down the post-mortem picture of the unidentified murder victim found on the beach. "Or this?" he asked, unfolding Mr Pettit's sketch.

"That poor girl," said Zimmerman indicating the photograph. "She looks bad, very poorly."

"But was it her who sold you the hat?"

"No, sorry. Never seen her before. Not this one, neither."

Wheatley was a little nonplussed. Was there a third mystery woman? "You said the girl who brought in the hat sold other things?"

"Just a few rags, a tattered old cloak, some holed stockings. Not worth anything really, but I am a soft touch. A sentimental old man."

"I'll need those as well," said Wheatley.

"Sorry, Mr Detective, already sold on. Will be ragged and off to the paper mill by now."

Hiding his disappointment, Wheatley said, "I'll just take the hat then, Mr Zimmerman."

"Call me Jakub. And you are young man?"

"Wheatley. Just Wheatley." Then realising that he was talking to someone he would almost certainly be seeing again in a professional way, "Detective Wheatley. I prefer Detective Wheatley, Mr Zimmerman."

Jakub Zimmerman looked down, slowly shook his head and said, "As you wish, Detective Wheatley." Picking up the hat, he blew softly on the ostrich feather, raising a cloud of dust, gently smoothed the plume with his free hand and said, "Your hat," passing it through the gap beneath the bars and placing it on the countertop.

"Thank you," said Wheatley.

"A very elegant hat," said Jakub. "Shall I add it to your account?"

"My account?"

The old man reached beneath the counter and brought out a pair of thick-lensed spectacles. Once these were settled on his nose to his satisfaction, he swivelled slowly on his stool, reached to the shelf behind him and took down a battered-looking tome. Opening the book, he licked the index finger of his left hand and paged through it. Finding the place he wanted, he ran his finger down the page at a snail's pace before saying, "Yes, here it is. Mr Wheatley." Jakub raised his head, lifted his spectacles to his forehead and gazed directly at the detective. "No initial," he said before snapping his spectacles back in place and continuing his perusal of the book. "Mr Wheatley. Sixth of February of this year. One cane, Malacca, silver-topped, iron ferrule. One pound, seventeen shillings and ninepence to be paid." Triumphantly Jakub ripped the spectacles from his face, slammed the account book shut and smiled at the detective.

"But that was seized as part of a police raid when a lot of stolen property was recovered."

Jakub Zimmerman maintained his smile. "The stick was stolen?"

"Well, no. That is, I'm not exactly sure. At present it has not been claimed as stolen."

The shop owner replaced his spectacles, opened the book, then reached beneath the counter to reveal a pen and ink-well. "Account it is," he said. "That will be eight shillings and sixpence for the hat, plus…"

"Wait a minute," said Wheatley. "Obviously I'll bring the cane back if it proves not to be stolen."

Jakub ceased his writing and pulled his spectacles further down his nose so that he could look over them at the increasingly frustrated detective. "I remember that cane. Such a stick. Such quality. I could allow you…" Jakub sucked on the end of his pen thoughtfully, then said, "I could give you as much as nineteen shillings, even possibly nineteen shillings and sixpence against your debt when you return the stick." He then dipped his pen in the ink and prepared to continue writing.

"You charged me far more than that for it," said Wheatley.

"Not charged," said Jakub Zimmerman. "We agreed a price between us and decided what it was worth to you. One pound, seventeen shillings and ninepence. To me, today, it's worth nineteen shillings and sixpence."

"So you say that even if I bring the cane back, I still owe you…" Here Wheatley's mathematics failed him, he was finding it difficult to think straight, and he settled for, "about eighteen shillings?"

"Eighteen shillings and threepence," corrected Jakub. "Plus interest," he added. "And eight shillings and sixpence for the hat."

"Interest?" spluttered Wheatley. The shop owner pointed with the end of his pen at a piece of card tied to the bars above the counter, which had '1¼% interest charged on ALL overdue accounts' printed untidily on it.

"So you're saying I owe eighteen and three plus 1¼%?"

Jakub was already reaching under the counter to emerge with an abacus and he proceeded to rapidly click balls backwards and forwards, saying, "1¼% interest per day, Detective Wheatley." Ceasing his rattling of the abacus he picked up a pen and wrote briefly in his book. "As of today you owe me one pound, nineteen shillings and twopence."

"Wait a moment," spluttered Wheatley.

"If I allow you, very generously I might add, nineteen shillings and sixpence against the return of the stick…"

Wheatley had had enough. "This is unacceptable," he said, turning on his heel to stalk out of the shop.

"Don't forget your hat, Detective Wheatley."

Wheatley snatched the hat off of the counter and stormed from the shop, leaving Jakub Zimmerman writing and saying aloud, "One lady's hat, ostrich feather, undamaged, eight shillings and sixpence."

Wheatley was almost back at the Town Hall before he realised that, in his confusion, he had forgotten to obtain a description of the woman who had sold the hat. He thought of returning but decided he would ask Sergeant Johnson to go to the pawnbroker's to get the description on Monday.

Monday 12th February 1894

The manager of the Royal Albion Hotel was not happy.

"You do realise that we have had to leave this room empty all weekend!"

Wheatley and Edwards continued to ignore him as they had ever since they had entered the room where Charlie Runcorn, known to the two detectives as Sir Tobias Hughes-Lewthwaite, baronet, had been found dead.

"And we've had to replace the mattress," continued the manager.

"Mattress was covered in blood when I arrived Friday," said Edwards to Wheatley. "Not much doubt about cause of death on this one."

"Who gave you permission to remove the mattress?" Edwards asked, turning to the hotel manager.

"Permission?" spluttered the manager. "We have guests arriving for this room this very afternoon. How could I not remove and replace it?"

Wheatley had searched the room thoroughly on arrival, finding only toiletries, some men's clothing amongst which was the Harris tweed suit he remembered 'Sir Toby' wearing, and an empty suitcase.

"Have you removed anything else?" he asked the manager.

"Only the sheets," he said, "and they had to be thrown away. No amount of washing would remove those stains." Here he actually shuddered. "Thank goodness the rest of the bedding was salvageable."

The room was on the second floor and its sea view overlooked the Fish Market and the construction site of the Brighton Marine Palace and Pier. Wheatley was taking in the view from the window, watching the thin snow falling. He kept his back to the manager as he asked, "When did you say the person calling himself Cecil de Vere arrived?"

He knew Edwards had already asked this on Friday last when he established the name used to book the room, so was unsurprised when the manager answered, "The gentleman arrived on Thursday morning." Wheatley was just about to dismiss the manager when he continued, "And Mrs de Vere arrived on Friday, just before lunch."

"Mrs de Vere?" said Edwards and Wheatley in unison.

"You said nothing about a Mrs de Vere," said Edwards.

"You didn't ask," sniffed the manager. Wheatley watched the manager calculating his response as Edwards moved swiftly towards him. He wisely decided his best move was to be co-operative. "Mr de Vere arrived on Thursday saying his wife had been delayed and would arrive the next day, which she did."

"No women's clothing left here," said Wheatley. "What happened to her luggage?"

"She didn't have any. I assumed Mr de Vere had brought her things with his."

Wheatley was pulling the photograph and the sketch of the two women involved in the case from his overcoat pocket. Replacing the photograph as he realised there was no point showing the likeness of the dead woman, he unfolded the sketch and offered it to the manager.

"Is this the woman you are referring to as Mrs de Vere?"

The manager took his time studying the drawing before saying, "No, I don't think so. The lady in question was, I would say, younger."

"So, what happened to her?"

"According to the desk clerk on duty she left about two o'clock saying she was off to do 'a bit of shopping'," said the manager. "She didn't return before the maid discovered the body at around four pm. And then there was such drama…"

"Such drama that you forgot all about her," said Edwards, before turning to Wheatley and saying, "I interviewed the maid. She saw nothing, did nothing. According to her, she used her pass key, meaning to deliver new towels when there was no answer to her knocking. She opened the door, saw the body, saw the blood, and ran screaming for the manager."

"I calmed her as best I could, then came to see for myself. I just stood in the doorway, ascertained the situation, relocked the door and went downstairs to telephone the police."

Wheatley turned back into the room and looked enquiringly at Edwards. Edwards shrugged so Wheatley said, "That's all, thank you."

"Unless you have anything else to add," he said to the manager as they left the room.

"There is one thing," the hotel manager said as he held the door for the two detectives, then lapsed into silence.

"We're waiting," growled Detective Edwards.

"Well, one learns never to pass comment on the guests, but Mrs de Vere…" Here he trailed off again.

"What about, Mrs de Vere?" prompted Wheatley.

"Mr de Vere was what you would call faded gentry. Good suit that has seen better times, handmade shoes polished to within an inch of their life. We get many of his sort here. The really rich ones go to the Grand, of course." The manager paused and seemed lost for a moment. Wheatley was about to prompt him again when he continued, "Mrs de Vere, her clothes were newer, but not quite of the quality a real lady would wear. And her accent was hardly upper class."

So much for not passing comment on the guests, thought Wheatley, before saying, "So perhaps you had doubts about her? Perhaps she wasn't quite what she seemed? Possibly not a married couple?"

"Oh no, nothing like that," blustered the manager. "We're not *that* sort of hotel. We always check that they're wearing a wedding ring." And with that he locked the room door and stalked off down the corridor.

Wheatley returned to the Police Station under the Town Hall having said goodbye to Detective Edwards, who had finished his shift. "Over an hour ago, Wheatley," he'd said. "Don't let me get into a habit of it, twelve hours is enough for one day, thirteen is too many." Wheatley was getting ready to set out for his appointment with Dr Barbara Buchanan when PC Jupp knocked on the door and entered the detective office.

"Mr Jupp," said Wheatley, "what can I do for you?"

"A small matter of a description by," here PC Jupp consulted his notebook, "Jakub Zimmerman, Pawnbroker, of New Road, Brighton."

"I thought Sergeant Johnson was going to deal with that."

"He did. He dealt with it by telling me to do it. Now, do you want to hear this description or not?"

Wheatley was a little taken aback. PC Jupp was a reliable and usually friendly police officer who he'd had many dealings with.

"Sorry, Mr Jupp, please go ahead."

"Won't do you much good, I'm afraid. Female wearing a dark coat and a hat of the type worn by almost every woman under sixty. Average height. Average weight. Dark hair. Aged anywhere between sixteen and twenty-five."

"That's a bit of a wide age range," said Wheatley.

"He said she was about the same age as his great-granddaughters," said Jupp, "but it turns out he's got seven of them, aged…"

"Between sixteen and twenty-five," interrupted Wheatley. "Did he say anything useful?"

"He did say she was, in his words…" another consultation of the notebook, "'a most attractive young lady with beautiful eyes like his wife's'. Not sure that's too helpful, not knowing his wife, like."

"Thank you anyway Mr Jupp. Sorry you had this put upon you."

PC Jupp was just leaving when he said, "Oh by the way. The old sod told me to tell you your account now stands at one pound, nineteen shillings and sevenpence halfpenny, plus eight and six for the hat, which will attract interest at $1\frac{1}{4}$% per diem from tomorrow."

"What did you say to that?" Wheatley asked faintly.

"I said he could push his account up his arse and unless he wanted Sergeant Johnson and his mates calling round to perform that service for him, he should keep quiet and show a bit of respect for the Constabulary." PC Jupp said this so casually that he could almost be reading aloud an official report. "I hope that was in order, Detective Wheatley."

It took an open-mouthed Wheatley a few seconds before he replied, "Yes, thank you, Mr Jupp, perfectly in order"

"Just saying what I'm sure you would have said if you was there, lad," said PC Jupp as he left the office.

It was a bemused Wheatley, chuckling to himself, who braved the cold and the snow as he set out to meet Dr Buchanan. He cut down to the seafront and walked along Madeira Road at the foot of the sea wall shielding the East Cliff. The snow he had observed from the window of the Royal Albion Hotel had worsened, driven by a cruel, easterly wind. Not the friendly, fluffy stuff beloved of children for their snow statues and snowball fights, but the wet stinging kind which reddened faces and seeped into shoes. Passing the Chain Pier, he was glad to get respite from the weather under the cover of the recently completed Madeira Terraces. The shelter continued until he reached the passenger lift which deposited him at the top of the cliff close to the Sussex County Hospital. Just before he reached the hospital, Wheatley turned right and gratefully entered the fug and warmth of the Sudely Arms. In the calm of the curtained entrance, he stamped his feet to loosen the ice crystals formed on his boots and shook the moisture from his bowler hat. Pushing through the curtain he checked Dr Buchanan's 'office' — the Snug Bar — but finding it empty, returned to the public bar.

"Constable. I hope it's nice to see you again."

The barman, Simon, who had been introduced to Wheatley during his previous visit, bustled along his side of the counter and looked quizzically at the young detective.

"I prefer Detective," said Wheatley, "Detective Wheatley. I'm here to see Dr Buchanan."

"Here to see the second-most-famous Dr Buchanan, how exciting."

"Second-most-famous Dr Buchanan?" said Wheatley.

"Well, I suppose she's the most famous Dr Buchanan now," said Simon, mopping the bar with a cloth he had pulled from the strings of his apron, "Sir James died a couple of years ago."

"Sir James?" said Wheatley.

"Honestly, I thought you was a detective. Sir James Buchanan? Chief Medical Officer of England? Ring a bell?"

"She's related to him?"

"So the rumour goes. Why else do you think this lot tolerate her?" Simon nodded to indicate the exclusively male clientele of the public bar. "But I'm not one for gossip, Detective. What'll you have? A nice sarsaparilla — no gin? I'll get the doc's Cognac while you think about it"

"Actually," said Wheatley, "I'll have a brandy too," adding, "I got quite chilled on the walk here," as a weak excuse.

Simon had already placed a brandy glass on the bar in front of him and now placed another beside it. Then he disappeared beneath the bar and re-emerged with an ancient-looking bottle from which he poured two generous measures. As Wheatley reached into his pocket to pay for the drinks, Simon held out a restraining hand.

"I'll put these on Dr Buchanan's account," he said, adding, "You couldn't afford them on your wages," as he scuttled to the other end of the bar to serve another customer, leaving Wheatley speechless.

Shaking his head, Wheatley carried the drinks into the Snug Bar and set them down on the familiar table beneath the mirror etched with an advertisement for Tamplin's Ales. The bar certainly lived up to its name with a glowing coal fire heating the small room, so Wheatley removed his overcoat and hung it up before settling at the table. Remembering the way Dr Buchanan had acted in appreciation of her brandy, he picked up his drink and cradled it in his hands. Lowering his head, he breathed in heavily over his glass, coughing and almost spilling the liquid as he inhaled the heady fumes.

"I see you're anticipating needing a pick-me-up *before* learning the gory details this time," said Dr Buchanan as she breezed into the room, shutting the door firmly behind her. "How are you, Wheatley?" asked the doctor as she removed her coat and placed it over the detective's on the coat stand. She didn't wait for a reply. Rapidly sitting opposite to him, she picked up her own drink and said, "Now, a lesson in the appreciation of a fine Cognac. Looks like you need it." Wheatley put his glass down and glanced up at the mirror wondering whether he had inadvertently got out of bed on the wrong side that morning the way he seemed to be treading on the toes of everyone he met today. As he returned his attention to her, Dr Buchanan was in full flow. "Pick up your glass, chop chop. Warm it between your hands like so." She held out her glass in both hands and waited until Wheatley followed her. "Now place the nose over the glass and breathe in. Gently. You're not sniffing back snot in church."

Wheatley had to prevent himself coughing again at the doctor's colourful phrase but had to admit that the warming fumes were most pleasant. He didn't remember this pleasure from the brandies he had drunk two nights ago.

"Now, take a sip. Just a small one and hold it in your mouth."

Wheatley complied.

"Breathing through your nose, allow the liquid to flow to the back of your tongue, across the tonsils, over the epiglottis, down the oesophagus and into the stomach."

Dr Buchanan closed her eyes and became intensely still as Wheatley experienced again the gentle warmth which had persuaded him that, although he disliked alcohol, he liked brandy.

"How was that?" asked Dr Buchanan, coming alive again.

"Wonderful," said Wheatley. "Though very different from other brandies I've had," he said, assuming the nonchalance of a connoisseur rather than the amateur with one horrific experience that he really was.

"You've probably had pub brandy, pure alcohol mixed with colouring. Caramel if you're lucky. Boot polish if you're not. This, on the other hand, is the finest Cognac from a single producer in the Charente." She looked at him expectantly. Wheatley thought she was probably talking about somewhere in France but couldn't be sure.

"Simon said it was very expensive," offered Wheatley.

"My treat, think nothing of it."

"He also said you were related to Sir James Buchanan, the old Chief Medical Officer."

"I don't like to speak of it," said Barbara Buchanan brusquely. "Suffice it to say that it suits my purpose if certain people believe that. Now are we here to gossip or shall we discuss my autopsy report?"

Wheatley read the report while Dr Buchanan appreciated her drink. Finishing, he extracted the post-mortem photograph of Charlie Runcorn, alias Cecil de Vere, alias Sir Tobias Hughes-Lewthwaite, and placed it in his jacket pocket with the picture of the murdered woman and the sketch of the disappeared 'Miss Stephanie'. He then looked up to ask a question but the doctor forestalled him.

"Drink up," she said, waving her empty glass. "We need at least another couple of these before we get down to it."

"I think I'll stick with this one," said Wheatley, not wishing to repeat the experience of two nights ago, or the bottle-ache of the following morning. "Thank you for the offer, though."

"Suit yourself," said Dr Buchanan, turning to press the service bell in the panelling behind her. Simon answered almost at once and while he left to fulfil the order, doctor and detective sat in silence.

After the delivery of her cognac, Dr Buchanan took a swift swallow with none of the finesse she had previously advocated before saying, "Sorry if I seem a bit bloody, Wheatley. Had an awful day once again justifying my existence. In truth, the autopsy was my high point. Now, questions?"

"You give cause of death as Syncope, which I understand completely because there was so much blood saturating the sheets of the bed he was found on that they had to be burned."

"Rupture of the femoral artery, that'll do it all right. Resulting from multiple stab wounds to the extreme lower abdomen and upper thigh."

"But you also say there is evidence of asphyxia, leading to loss of consciousness, like the woman found on the beach."

"Yes, ligature marks around the throat. However, this time it is certain that it was the loss of blood that caused death. He wouldn't have bled anywhere near as much if it had been the throttling that killed him."

"So some similarities between the two deaths," Wheatley mused aloud.

"I'd say more than some," said the doctor, "In my opinion it was the same modus operandi, ergo the same murderer."

"But there was much more evidence of stabbing in this case."

"Not so, it just happens that the bleeding was external this time."

"So possibly the same person killed him as killed my mystery woman."

"A certainty, I'd say."

Dr Buchanan went on to emphasise the similarities in the two cases: no defence wounds, both throttled to unconsciousness with the same pair of ligature marks caused by a flat narrow material, both multiple stabbings to the lower abdomen using a long, extremely thin, circular, blade.

"Well," said Wheatley as she finished, "if you are right, we seem to have a double murderer on our hands. And I have to confess I don't know where to look. I just hope it doesn't escalate like the Whitechapel murders."

Dr Buchanan had finished her drink and fetched her coat. "Heaven forbid," she said, "but I have complete faith in you, Wheatley. As for where to look, I'd *cherchez la femme* if I were you."

Wheatley mouthed the unfamiliar words as she continued. "Think about it. Victim one: attractive young woman. Pregnant. Killed by internal bleeding from a frenzied attack to the area of her womb. Victim two: older man purporting to be rich and powerful. Killed by external bleeding from a frenzied attack to the area of his groin."

"Yes?" said Wheatley

"His sexual organs and her reproductive ones were the objects of attack. Sounds like a crime of passion to me. Mark my words, there's a woman involved."

"But surely a woman wouldn't do such a thing. Or have the strength to do it."

"Don't be naïve, Wheatley." Doctor Barbara had sat down again. "We women aren't the sweet wilting flowers you seem to think we are. And we're a lot stronger than we look."

"But," she continued as the detective looked at her quizzically, "I have to admit that there is a problem with a woman throttling a man, particularly a rather big man like the victim. Unconsciousness isn't immediate. Even if attacked suddenly from behind he'd still have had time to reach behind and wrestle for control of the material looped round his neck. It would have to be an unusually strong woman to best a man at that contest."

"So, your theory of a female murderer has flaws. In fact, it's unlikely. Very unlikely," said Wheatley.

"Yes," said the doctor, "I suppose that's why you're the detective and I'm just the pathologist."

Dr Buchanan had put on her coat and was checking her appearance in the mirror, re-pinning her hat more firmly on her fashionably piled hair.

"So no suspects, male or female?"

"Not a suspect as such, but we still haven't found the missing woman whose disappearance began this whole investigation." Wheatley reached into his pocket and took out the artist's impression of 'Miss Stephanie'. Could she really be a murderess? Surely not. No, out of the question. But Dr Barbara's suggestion was tugging at something in his memory. He was so absorbed in his thoughts that he

131

hardly noticed when the drawing was pulled from his fingers, looking up to see Dr Buchanan perusing the picture, her brow furrowed.

"Strange picture," she said. "You're sure this is a good likeness?"

"As sure as I can be," said Wheatley. "Why do you ask?"

"Nothing certain, but the composition of the face doesn't look natural. And the features seem too regular. How did you obtain it?"

"It was compiled by an artist from a witness' description," said Wheatley, taking the drawing back from the doctor.

"Probably that explains it," she said.

"Almost certainly," said Wheatley.

"Even so…" said Dr Buchanan. Then with a facial change from a frown to a smile and a cheery, "Must be off," she left Wheatley alone in the snug. In the back of his mind, something was niggling at him as he wondered just how expensive this wonderfully warming Cognac was.

Tuesday 13th February 1894

"Ah, there you are, Whatley. Found the so-called Sir Tobias, I see."

Wheatley had spent most of the day trying to piece together his case which was growing ever more complicated. When he was sent for by the Inspector, he had feared the worst, expecting to be reprimanded at the very least for his sojourn to Marylebone and his skirmish with the Metropolitan Police. He was relieved to see that this did not seem to be the purpose of the summons. Not only was the Inspector sitting at his desk rather than his preferred armchair by the fire, but he was intently studying the file Wheatley had sent up to him that afternoon.

"You consider the murderer to be the same as the woman found on the beach?"

"Yes, sir. Dr Buchanan was clear that the method appeared the same."

"Ah, yes, Dr Buchanan. You trust her judgement, do you?" The inspector looked from the file directly at Wheatley. "I mean, a woman doctor. Hardly likely to be the right kind of person for this sort of thing, don't you think?"

Considering that the first victim was female and pregnant, Wheatley believed that a female physician was exactly the right kind of person for this sort of thing, but he held his council. No answer was necessary as the Inspector continued.

"Well bred, though," he said.

"Sir?" said Wheatley.

"Breeding, Constable. Comes of good stock. Rides with the Goodwood I hear."

"Goodwood?"

"The Goodwood Hunt, Whatley." The Inspector had gone back to studying the file. "I don't suppose you've been blooded?" he said looking up.

Wheatley was becoming confused at the turn of the conversation, but fortunately it seemed an answer was not expected and the Inspector continued on more familiar ground.

"So, what's your theory, young man?"

"Well, sir, I was wondering whether Sir Toby had annoyed someone he had tried to part from his money," said Wheatley.

"More than likely," replied Inspector Cronin.

"Exactly," said Wheatley. "So I thought if I could interview, the members of your... er, club. Just the ones closest to Sir Toby, of course."

"My club?"

"Your... Lodge," said Wheatley. "Detective Winstanley told me about your... society."

"Well, he shouldn't have. Really what is the world coming to? First a charlatan taking advantage of his presumed status. Now a fellow traveller disclosing a gentleman's private business. Where will it end, I ask myself?" The inspector had stood, pushing his chair back and resting his hands on the desk either side of the open file.

"I do need to talk to all those involved, sir."

"What do you mean, involved?"

The inspector held his hand out as Wheatley prepared to answer. "Surely you see this is impossible, Wheatley? No, it won't do. These are gentlemen of the highest calibre. Peers of the realm. Judges and Queen's Councils. Eminent professors. There is no way I can permit them to be questioned by a mere…"

"But sir, this is a double murder enquiry. Not to mention a disappearance and a perpetual fraudster."

"I said *no*, Wheatley."

Angry as he was at another block in the way of his enquiry, Wheatley didn't miss the fact that the Inspector had used his correct name twice in a row, nor the word 'mere'. He stood seething, his eyes fixed to the wall just to the right of the Inspector's head. There was a moment of impasse before the Inspector spoke in a more moderate tone.

"I shall, of course have to appraise the gentlemen concerned of Sir Tobias' trickery. And the more welcome news that he has met his just deserts. At that time, I shall make discreet enquiries and if I find anything pertaining to the case, I shall of course inform you."

The Inspector paused and looked expectantly at Wheatley.

"Thank you, sir." Wheatley supplied the expected response.

"Very well. That will be all, Whatley."

"Wheatley, sir," said Wheatley automatically as he left the room.

Wednesday 14th February 1894

Wheatley had spent a frustrating two days trying to locate two mystery women and identify the murdered girl. He had failed. He was sitting at the desk in the Detective Office with the post-mortem photographs of the two murder victims and the sketch of the missing Miss Stephanie when Detective Edwards breezed in ready for his late shift.

"You're looking particularly morose today, Wheatley. Cheer up, it's only a job."

"That's the problem; it isn't, is it?" said Wheatley without looking up, still gazing at the pictures in front of him. "I've a murderer on the loose, a missing girl to find and a so-called wife of one of the victims who is certainly a witness if not worse but who has also disappeared."

Edwards had moved to the coat stand to hang his hat. He then removed Wheatley's jacket from the coat hanger where it was neatly stored while the detective was at his desk and held it out, ready to be put on.

"You won't get anywhere sitting there going round in circles. Come on, get your hat and coat on and go home. Tomorrow is another day," said Edwards.

Wheatley removed the sleeve-holders used to hitch up his shirt cuffs to prevent any chance of them getting ink-stained, then did up the two bottom buttons of his waistcoat which he always unfastened when seated to stop it creasing. While Wheatley was shrugging into his jacket, Edwards asked if he could do anything to help.

"You could check that the descriptions of the two women are still being circulated by the constables on the beat," said Wheatley, winding his scarf around his neck before encasing himself in his overcoat. "If there's any trace, any clue at all, make sure you send a message to my lodgings and I'll be in at once."

"Don't you worry about that," said Edwards. "Off you go home. You could do with a rest."

"Not just yet," said Wheatley. "I called earlier at the house on the Steyne but there was no answer, so I'm off to try again."

"Ah, not rest but recreation in the hands of the lovely Millie," said Edwards. "Just as good and very appropriate."

"Not at all," said Wheatley. "It occurred to me today that we've been ignoring the Garsons in this case. After all, they knew the missing girl and one of the victims, so I want to talk to them again. Also, I want to take another look at the missing woman's bedroom. There's a nagging at the back of my mind about something Dr Buchanan said, but I can't tie it down." Wheatley took his hat from the rack and was about to leave when he said, "What do you mean, 'very appropriate'?"

"Well, it is St Valentine's Day," grinned Edwards.

"What has that got to do with anything?" said Wheatley, leaving the room.

As Wheatley approached across the Steyne, Number 28, Grand Parade seemed in darkness. Resigning himself to the lack of success he had experienced all day, he was about to climb the short flight of steps to the front door just in case the house was occupied when he noticed a glow from below. Crouching to look through the basement window, he saw Millie sitting at the kitchen table illuminated by an oil lamp. *At least there's someone at home this time*, he thought as he descended the steps to the tradesman's entrance and rapped on the door.

"Detective," squealed Millie. "Come in. Want a sherry?" Wheatley followed Millie into the kitchen where she plonked herself down on a chair behind the table. "I'm so glad you came to see me," she said.

"Actually," said Wheatley, eyeing the half empty bottle of sherry beside the completely empty glass on the table in front of Millie, "it's the Garsons I've come to see."

"Oh them," said Millie, refilling her glass. "They left ages ago. Gone home."

"Left?" said Wheatley. "When?"

"That day I went with you to see the body. I told you."

"You definitely did not tell me; I'd have made a note of it."

"Well, I thought I did. What does it matter anyway?"

"It matters because I want to talk to them," said Wheatley. "You said they'd gone home. Where is home?"

"I don't know. Kent somewhere."

"You don't know the address, I suppose? Or even the town would help."

"No I don't," said Millie. "And if that's all you've come here for, you can leave now."

"It wasn't just for that," said Wheatley, wondering why Millie was upset and putting it down to the wine she was drinking. "I also need another look at Miss Stephanie's bedroom. Something I need to check."

This seemed, surprisingly, to placate Millie, who smiled and said, "Well, you'll need a drink first."

"I don't drink," said Wheatley.

"That's not what the state you were in when I saw you last Saturday suggests," said Millie. "Nor the stories that nice Mr Pettit told while we were making that drawing. The least you can do tonight is have a drink with me." She held up the sherry bottle, eyebrows raised.

Wheatley was appalled at Pettit's indiscretion but considered that the easiest way out of this impasse was capitulation. One small drink and he could complete his inspection of Miss Stephanie's room and possibly get home for supper.

"I only drink brandy," said Wheatley.

"We got that!" said Millie, rising and heading towards the arch separating the kitchen from the storage areas. "Take your coat off and sit down."

"Only Cognac, not the ordinary stuff," said Wheatley hastily.

"We got that, too," said Millie, disappearing into the gloom.

Wheatley placed his hat and scarf on the table, removed his topcoat and looked around for somewhere to hang it, eventually having to drape it across the back of one of the chairs. Then he took a seat opposite to where Millie had been sitting and wracked his brains to try to sort out what was niggling him about Miss Stephanie's bedroom.

Millie was gone some time. When she returned, she entered the kitchen via the door which Wheatley knew from his previous visit led to the stairs to the upper portion of the house. She held a lit candle in a holder in one hand and a bottle in the other.

"How did you do that?" he said.

"Used the back stairs like a good servant is supposed to," she said. "But I came back down the proper ones. This do? I had to burgle Sir Toby's drinks cupboard to get it." She set the candle down beside the oil lamp on the table and held out the bottle towards Wheatley. "Can't make head or tail of it myself. What's it say?"

Wheatley looked at the label on the bottle which seemed to be handwritten in a language he assumed to be French. At the Catholic school he had attended periodically, Wheatley had studied Latin, of course. And once they realised his intelligence, some classical Greek, despite him being precluded from studying for the priesthood by his half Hebrew background. He also had a smattering of Yiddish provided by his mother. But no French. However, he could clearly see the word 'Cognac' on the label and looking up to see Millie's expectant face surprised himself by bluffing. "First class. From a single vineyard on the Charente."

"Oooh, Detective," said Millie, obviously impressed.

Her reaction caused Wheatley to go further.

"Call me Wheatley, everyone does," he said.

"I prefer Detective. More manly somehow," said Millie, placing two tumblers on the table and half filling them with the brandy. "Chin, chin."

"What's the matter?" she said, noticing Wheatley had only sipped at his Cognac while she had finished hers.

"Wrong glasses," said Wheatley.

"What do you mean?"

"Cognac should be served in balloon glasses so that the vapours can accumulate." Wheatley was drawing on his lessons from Dr Buchanan.

"Vapours, eh?" said Millie, taking up the candle again. "You mean them great big round glasses? There are some upstairs. You finish that while I go and get them," and she disappeared through the door.

"Now let's have them vapours," said Millie after she had returned with two enormous brandy glasses which Wheatley had to prevent her from filling to the brim.

"Firstly," said Wheatley, "Warm the Cognac with the glass between your hands before inhaling gently..."

"Aaah, gets right up me nose," giggled Millie the first time she inhaled and she snorted loudly. By the second glass, Wheatley was pleased to see that his tutelage was bearing fruit and Millie becoming more adept. However, the drink seemed to be making her clumsy. Three times now her knee had touched his under the table and he had had to take avoiding action. So, after the third glass, he decided that he had fulfilled any social obligations and could get back to police work.

"Very pleasant," he said. "But now I really must be going. I just need to take a look at that bedroom first."

"Righto," said Millie, jumping up and not seeming at all displeased at him curtailing his visit. "I'll go up and light the lamp. I can find my way all right in the dark. You follow on with the candle." Then, picking up their two empty glasses and opening the door to the stairs she said, "I've got these, you bring the bottle."

Thursday 15ᵗʰ February 1894

Weak daylight was filtering between the curtains. Wheatley lifted his head from the pillow and immediately closed his eyes. The unfortunately familiar somersault in his stomach and beating pulse in his temples caused him to lie back slowly and reflect that once again he had succumbed to the dreaded bottle-ache. Realising that he had no memory whatsoever of how he had got back to his lodgings and hoping he had not disgraced himself he slowly raised himself to a sitting position and swung his legs to the floor. Opening his eyes, he was relieved to see that he was not fully dressed as last time. But he was not wearing his night shirt. *I seem to have slept in my underwear*, he thought, looking down at that week's woollen combinations. As he became more awake, he realised that the bottle-ache was nowhere as severe as last time. Perhaps he hadn't drunk that much after all? Or perhaps the better quality of Cognac over brandy mitigated it somewhat? As he mused over this, he couldn't help a feeling that something was wrong. That the room felt and sounded different. And then, just as he lurched to his feet, realising that the feeling of wrongness was caused by there being someone else in the room, a dazzling burst of sunlight caused him to slam his eyes shut again and sink back onto the bed.

"Good morning," said a voice that he hoped he didn't recognise but had to accept that he did. As he cracked open his eyelids, he saw a shadowed figure standing by the curtains which she had just opened causing the dazzling sunlight. Surely a dream! What was Millie doing in his bedroom? And then he realised that this wasn't his bedroom. That it wasn't a dream. And that he was sitting on a bed that wasn't his, in a room that wasn't his, in his combinations. And in the presence of a female. Looking around frantically, he spied his clothes folded neatly on the stool to the dressing table which was unmistakably the dressing table in Sir Tobias's bedroom.

Wheatley hurled himself to his feet and grabbed his shirt from the pile of clothing and held it out to conceal as much of his underwear as possible from the feminine gaze, thanking his forethought in paying the additional sixpence and purchasing a shirt with the extra-long tails.

"Bit late for that isn't it, Detective?" said Millie.

Wheatley had no idea what to say to this but resolutely held the shirt in front of him as a shield. Then Millie moved into the light and he realised that beneath the shawl wrapped around her shoulders to protect her from the morning chill, she was wearing the embroidered apricot nightdress. The shift which she had draped provocatively around herself on his first visit when investigating Miss Stephanie's disappearance. And in the morning light pouring through the east facing window, it was just as translucent as he had thought it would be. Now he was doubly glad that he was holding his linen shield.

"I've put a cup of tea on the table there for you," said Millie. "Hurry up and get dressed. We'll have breakfast downstairs."

Wheatley was having trouble thinking, let alone speaking but he somehow made it understood that breakfast would not be necessary.

"Nonsense," said Millie making her way to the bedroom door. "You can't go to work on an empty stomach."

"You *are* going to work today, aren't you?" she said as she left the room.

*

"So that explains the late arrival and the lack of hat and overcoat," said Edwards placing a glass of foaming Emerson's Bromo Selzer in front of his young colleague. "You just up and left? No goodbye or nothing?"

"I couldn't think what else to do," said a miserable Wheatley.

"And you don't remember anything about the night before?"

"Nothing after leaving the kitchen."

"Oh, bad luck," said Edwards. "Not even a little?"

"No," said Wheatley. "And that's what's strange."

"How do you mean?" asked Edwards. "After all, you're not used to drink and the same thing happened to you when you went out with that London Police fellow."

"Winstanley, yes," said Wheatley. "But that's what is worrying me. Though I said last time I couldn't remember anything, actually I could. A little. I had confused flashbacks or memories that might have been dreams. Or nightmares. Just a few seconds here and there. But I remembered some details. Last night is a complete blank. No flashbacks. No dreams. Nothing."

"But you must have…" He paused. Wheatley was slumped at the desk, his hands over his eyes, obviously distraught. "Here, here," said Edwards. "It's not that bad. A bit of a caddish thing to just leave without a goodbye, but that can be put right. Bunch of flowers. Box of sweetmeats. That sort of thing. Pity about missing out on a fried breakfast, though."

"It's just that if I… I don't know what to do. How to act. I'm not sure I'm ready to get married yet, but obviously…"

"Now, now, wait just a minute," interrupted Edwards. "What's this about? Valentine's evening. A pretty girl. A few drinks. A few more drinks. No need to start talking about matrimony. Just chalk it up to experience."

"That's not easy when you haven't any."

"Any what?"

"Experience." Now he'd begun Wheatley couldn't seem to stop himself. "That is, I've never…"

"Never?"

147

"Never."

"But you must have," said Edwards. "At your age!"

Then, as Wheatley once again lapsed into miserable silence, he heard Edwards say, "How old *are* you anyway?"

"Twenty-three last August."

"Hang on, that can't be right," said Edwards. "I know they were asking for at least ten years' experience when they advertised for a detective."

"Yes, well," said Wheatley. "My parents died when I was twelve, just after I'd left school. A relative of my mother's — my uncle, I suppose, though he never acknowledged me, presumably because of my gentile blood — lived in Brunswick Town. They had their own watch and I moved into the Watch House on Brunswick Square. The watch operated twenty-four hours a day and they needed someone to keep the fire burning, the lamps trimmed, the tea hot. I had a roof over my head and made a few pennies cleaning boots, so I survived well enough. Then, when I was seventeen, I was 'promoted' to apprentice constable. I still had to keep the fire burning, the lamps trimmed, the tea hot, but I also got the night patrols. You know, the ones in the dog hours when every right-thinking person, even those with criminal intent, are snug in their beds snoring while I interminably patrolled the deserted streets, checked doors were locked and shivered in the biting wind off the sea. I was bored but something about service as a policeman got to me. I wanted to make a difference. Do some real policing. Solve

148

actual crimes rather than looking for lost dogs. So, when the Brighton Constabulary advertised they were expanding their detective force…"

"Expanding," snorted Edwards. "One more poor sod to be given all the stuff no one else could be bothered to solve."

"Anyway," Wheatley continued, "by the time I applied, strictly speaking, I had been associated with a police force for over ten years. I just didn't mention what I did or how young I'd been when I started.

"And left the word 'apprentice' off of the form," added Wheatley after a pause.

"They never checked," after a further pause.

"Lazy buggers," said Edwards. "Still, not like you, Wheatley, to be inexact with the truth."

"It was wrong, yes. I just so wanted to make people's lives better. At least that's how I justified it to myself," said Wheatley. He sat, eyes cast down, feeling as if one unhappiness was piling upon another. "It is said that your sins will find you out and mine certainly have. I suppose it's all over now. Being a detective, I mean."

"Not unless you want it to be, lad," said Edwards. "I'm no nark and us plainclothes men need to stick together. As far as I'm concerned, you're a young-looking colleague about ten years younger than me. And yes, that does make me forty next birthday."

"You don't look it."

"Was that a smile?" said Edwards. "Right, this is what we're going to do. Firstly we are going to play on Sergeant

Johnson's non-existent feelings to borrow the razor and shaving things he keeps beneath his desk. Then, after your ablutions, I am going to escort you to number 28, Grand Parade. You will go in alone. You will apologise to the young lady and admit that you acted like an idiot."

"An idiot?" said Wheatley.

"Idiotically. And caddishly. Then you will state that you cannot remember anything about last night, ascertain the facts, retrieve your hat and coat..."

"And scarf," said Wheatley.

"If you must," said Edwards. "Retrieve your hat, coat *and* scarf, claim pressure of work and leave, promising whatever you must to make the situation better. I'll be waiting outside and once you have acquainted me with the facts, we can decide a plan of action together."

"I couldn't just write her a letter?" asked Wheatley.

Friday 16th February 1894

Wheatley was thinking about the conversation with Millie when he had returned hatless and coatless to the house on the Steyne. She had stood in the open door, his hat, coat and scarf in her hands. As he had taken them and thanked her, he had tried to form the words his racing brain were concocting but he could find none that were suitable. Well, not suitable, but respectful enough to establish what he needed to know. Instead, a gush of babble came out as he struggled into his overcoat and wound his scarf. Millie just stood holding his hat until he came to an embarrassed silence. As she presented him with his bowler, she used her other hand to place her fingers over his lips.

"Don't worry about it, Detective," was all she said. Retreating inside, she called, "Stay for breakfast next time," closing the door and leaving Wheatley on the doorstep, confused and none the wiser.

Since then, Wheatley had to reappraise his complete knowledge of the female sex and of the morals drummed into him by both of his religions. It was universally accepted that any relations with the fairer sex were conducted within marriage. Of course, he knew that there was an underclass of women who, through poverty or extraneous circumstances, catered to men's brutish urges for money. Some were even reputed to enjoy it! But not nice girls. Not girls it was possible to marry. Not women like his mother. Or Mrs Harris or Mrs Lee. Not girls like Millie. Or so he had thought. Had he misjudged her? Or was society different to the way he was brought up to believe? Were the stories circulated by the younger constables not, as he had thought the smutty imaginings of rough fellows, but the true state of affairs?

He was so confused and had so many thoughts spinning round his head that he almost missed it. He had consulted Kelly's Gazetteer of Sussex, 1893 edition, and found seven letting agencies listed in the Steyne area in his effort to establish the whereabouts of the Garsons. He knew from Millie that they had returned to their house in Kent, but she could not tell him the address. Wheatley had visited six letting agents so far today and his feet were aching. None of them was the agent for 28, Grand Parade. The seventh was impossible to find. Despite having been printed clearly in the Gazetteer, the address appeared to be that of a private house. It was only as he decided to give up and call it a day that he noticed the twitten separating the house from its neighbour. Moving a little way along the narrow passageway he spied a door with an impressively painted board attached to it saying, 'Regency Letting Agency: Comfortable Holiday Dwellings for Gentlefolk, Fully Serviced.' There was no bell or knocker and so Wheatley pushed gently on the door. It opened onto a flight of stairs. On the wall a notice showed an arrow pointing upwards. Underneath someone had written 'Regency Lettings; three flights up'.

The three flights were long and very steep. Wheatley was quite out breath when he reached the ultimate landing beneath a skylight which illuminated only dimly, having been almost obscured by bird droppings. The single door facing him had a frosted glass window on which 'Regency Letting Agency' had been elegantly sign-written. Below the word 'Proprietor' was in the same refined hand but the original name had been obscured by a piece of paper pasted over it. Handwritten on the piece of paper was the name James Coughlin Esq.

Pausing a moment to catch his breath, Wheatley opened the door and entered a small ante-room. There was barely room for the desk, behind which sat a lady whose age Wheatley estimated to be well beyond sixty years. Whilst she was immaculately dressed, her age was matched by her couture, her clothing being reminiscent of a bygone era.

"Can I help you?" she asked, rising to her feet. This seemed to cause a small tremor through the room, her chair slamming into the wall behind and her shoulders brushing the two filing cabinets on each side of her.

"I'm making enquiries about number 28, Grand Parade," said Wheatley. "Do you by any chance represent the owners?"

"We do indeed," said the woman. "If you will wait here for a moment, please, sir, I shall ascertain whether Mr Coughlin is free."

So saying, she squeezed from behind her desk and passed through a door opposite to the one Wheatley had entered by. She closed the door behind her and left Wheatley wondering which law of nature it was that decided that it was always the last place one tried that yielded results.

Within a few moments the woman returned and stood holding the door open, indicating that Wheatley should enter. The office beyond showed evidence of once being that of a prosperous businessman. It was well proportioned and light from a large window illuminated the expensive, but extremely old fashioned, furniture. However, the carpet was worn and the wallpaper faded, brighter squares showing where pictures had once hung. The man who approached Wheatley from behind the desk which dominated the room was young, perhaps only a couple of years older than Wheatley himself. In contrast to his colleague, he was dressed in the latest fashion. His suit was a light grey and his waistcoat checked, while a stick-pin, its 'diamond' too large to be real, anchored his yellow tie. His gaudy apparel was matched by the enthusiasm with which he pumped Wheatley's hand.

"Coughlin, proprietor of Regency Lettings for my sins. Miss Yardley informs me you are interested in 28, Grand Parade. You are a lucky man, sir, it has just become available." Placing a chair in front of the desk he continued, "If you will take a seat, sir, we can arrange a viewing."

Wheatley remained standing. At the man's quizzical look he said, "I'm afraid we seem to be at cross purposes, Mr Coughlin. Let me introduce myself. Detective Wheatley, Brighton Municipal Constabulary. I'm here to enquire of the whereabouts of two employees of yours. A Mr and Mrs Garson."

Mr Coughlin's demeanour changed instantly and he slumped down in the chair he had arranged for Wheatley. "It's that woman," he said. "Always getting things wrong. She distinctly said you were here about a letting. She's as old as Methuselah. I inherited her when I took over the firm from my Great-Uncle just before he died. I suppose I ought to let her go but I don't have the heart to."

"Yes, well," said Wheatley. "About the Garsons."

"Yes, the Garsons." Mr Coughlin seemed to be getting more morose by the minute. "What have they done, now?"

"Nothing as far as I know," said Wheatley, filing away the 'done now' remark in his memory. "I just need to speak to them about an ongoing enquiry and I understand they have returned to their home."

"Yes, we employ people such as the Garsons part-time only. Usually just for the season. It was a slice of luck that the lessor wished to stay on during the winter."

"So, if you could supply the Garsons' address?" said Wheatley.

"Yes, of course," said Mr Coughlin, standing. "I must also check that Miss Yardley remembered to send out a reminder about the overdue rent on number 28."

"Ah," said Wheatley. "I regret to inform you that the person you knew as Sir Tobias Hughes-Lewthwaite was found dead in the Royal Albion Hotel last Friday."

"Dead?" Mr Coughlin dropped himself back onto the seat of the chair.

"Yes, I'm investigating his murder."

"Murder?"

Wheatley waited for a while to allow the lettings agent to get over his shock. When there was no sign of this happening, he prompted gently, "The Garsons? Their address?"

Mr Coughlin rose and walked to the office door. Opening it he called, "Can you bring me in the file for 28, Grand Parade, please, Miss Yardley." He returned to sit down, behind the desk this time. "He owed me more than fifty pounds in rent!"

"Still, I daresay the estate will be good for it," he said brightening slightly.

Wheatley was wondering whether to disabuse him of his hopes and had decided not to depress the poor man even further when Miss Yardley entered and placed a folder on the desk in front of Mr Coughlin.

"Yes, here we are," he said, opening the file and consulting a slip of paper. "Micah Garson and wife. Footman and Cook. Address: 5, New Road, Shoreham."

"That sounds about right," said Wheatley, who was almost sure that there was a village called Shoreham in Kent.

"Yes, they live in when I have work for them but presumably have their own lodging for when I don't. Number 28, Grand Parade is empty now, of course."

"Well, apart from the maid," said Wheatley.

Mr Coughlin had closed the file and handed it back to his secretary.

"Thank you, Miss Yardley," he said before turning to Wheatley and saying, "Maid, what maid?"

"Millie," said Wheatley, then "Miss Millicent Stephens," as he heard the door shutting behind Miss Yardley.

"Never heard of her. And we don't employ maids, just a footman and cook. If they want maids, they have to supply their own."

"But..." said Wheatley before Mr Coughlin interrupted him.

"I can assure you that the house is locked up tight and will be until the Season begins. I checked it personally on my way in this morning. Now, unless there's anything else, Detective..."

The door closed behind him and Wheatley was navigating the few crowded steps to the outer door when he became aware that Miss Yardley was waving a handkerchief. Cursing himself for his bad manners — his confusion was no excuse — he turned towards the lady and touched the brim of his hat as a farewell gesture.

"Wait," said Miss Yardley. "Did I hear you ask about a maid, Mr..."

"Wheatley," said Wheatley, "Detective Wheatley, Brighton Municipal Constabulary. And you are Miss Yardley. I am sorry we weren't introduced. I was surprised to hear that you do not provide maids." Wheatley would have continued but Miss Yardley broke in.

"We used to. In the old days when the business was owned by Mr Owens. And before that by his father, old Mr Owens. When fully serviced accommodation *meant* fully serviced. We catered for real quality persons then."

"But not now?"

"Charlatans and ruffians since *he* jumped into the late Mr Owens' shoes." Miss Yardley's stare in the direction of Mr Coughlin's office left it in no doubt who *he* was.

"Surely not," said Wheatley. "After all, one needs a certain means to be able to lease such a property as 28, Grand Parade."

"I suppose so," said Miss Yardley. "Rich our current clients might be, but they are not what I would call refined." This was accompanied by a sharp nod of her head.

There was a short silence before Wheatley said, "No maids nowadays, you say. So you haven't heard of a Miss Millicent Stephens."

"Oh, but I have," said Miss Yardley. "We used to have a maid of that name working for us. Millie, we called her. Came from a farming family, if I remember rightly. Just a moment." Miss Yardley stood to pull out a filing drawer and take out a folder.

"Yes, here we are. Millicent Stephens. Ladies' maid. Address: Meadow Farm, Hassocks. Worked for us for six years. Pretty girl. And very personable. Some said a little *too* outgoing, but I liked her. That's why I remember her so well."

"Does she still work for you?" asked Wheatley. He recognised the description and wondered if the old lady was getting her times mixed up.

"Oh no. Not since it happened about ten years ago. So sad."

"Sad?" said Wheatley.

"She died, Detective. Such a lovely girl. Such a waste."

*

Back at the Town Hall Police Station, Wheatley was reviewing the case. Miss Yardley could throw no more light on the death of the ladies' maid, saying that she thought it was 'some sort of accident.' And she was adamant that Millicent Stephens died ten years ago, aged around twenty. Which meant, if true, his Millie would have been about nine years old at the time. Wheatley had sent a telegram to the Kent Constabulary asking them to confirm that the Garsons were resident at 5, New Road, Shoreham, before he made the long journey to interview them. In the meantime, he resolved to visit Meadow Farm early the following week to check Miss Yardley's recollection of Millicent Stephens. The name was

159

probably just a coincidence. Or, more likely the receptionist had become confused and was recollecting a different person altogether. She was rather ancient, after all.

Monday 19ᵗʰ February 1894

"You look worried," said Edwards as he breezed into the Detective Office to begin his shift. Wheatley was gazing at a telegram that had just been delivered. He placed it carefully on the desk in front of him and began to acquaint his colleague on his visit to the Regency Letting Agency.

"Always the last place you look," said Edwards. "So apart from your lady friend being a ghost, what else is worrying you?"

"She's not..." began Wheatley, meaning to say, 'not my lady friend', but considering recent circumstances changed to "...not a ghost, of course. The lady at the agency was obviously mistaken. I'll check it out tomorrow."

He pointed to the telegram on the desk.

"Then there's this," he said. "Kent Constabulary say there is no New Road in Shoreham. So now we've got the Garsons missing."

"Or hiding," said Edwards. "You did say they might be suspects."

"Missing suspects. How can we find them if we can't even find Miss Stephanie *or* the identity of the murdered woman?"

Edwards had picked up the telegram.

"Well, they're wrong about this. The wife's brother lives in Shoreham. I'm pretty sure New Road runs parallel to the High Street."

"Your wife comes from Kent?" asked Wheatley.

"No, Shoreham. On the Steyning line. About five miles west of Brighton."

"But this is about Shoreham in Kent," said Wheatley, removing the telegram from Edwards' grasp. "Millie said the Garsons lived in Kent."

"Yes, but why?" asked Edwards. "Why would someone live so far away from where they work? Surely it's more likely they would live closer. Did the gent from the letting agency definitely say Shoreham, Kent?"

"No," said Wheatley, "but..."

"There you are then, if it had been the Kentish Shoreham, he would have said so. He wouldn't say 'Shoreham, Sussex', though, because everyone knows that Shoreham is just along the road from here." Edwards looked very satisfied with his reasoning, spoiling it by adding, "Everyone but you, seemingly."

"But Millie said..."

"What have you got to lose by checking?" asked Edwards.

"I suppose I should," said Wheatley with no enthusiasm.

"That's the ticket," said Edwards. "To quote our illustrious Inspector, leave no stone unturned."

Tuesday 20th February 1894.

Wheatley arrived at Hassocks Railway Station and made his way along the High Street looking for the Post Office. He was glad to get inside out of the perpetual drizzle. The weather had become a little warmer, but that just meant wet sleet and snow had been replaced by even wetter drizzle and rain. A brief conversation with the Postmaster informed him that Meadow Farm was beyond Keymer on the Ditchling road.

"Be'n't no more'n a couple of miles over the fields. You'm able to walk it in half an hour, young bloke like you," Wheatley was told. When he expressed doubts about finding the way the Postmaster suggested he try the blacksmith. "Ol' George, he'll run you there in his pony'n'trap fer a shillin'."

The blacksmith's shop was a few steps along the High Street on the opposite side of the road to the Post Office and Wheatley found the blacksmith more than willing to drive him to the farm. It took a while for George to harness up and Wheatley basked in the heat from the forge while he waited.

"You'm ready then?" called the blacksmith.

Reluctantly, Wheatley left the shelter of the shop and headed for the pony and trap. Mercifully the rain had stopped but the weather was still raw. George silently handed him two old sacks as he prepared to climb into the carriage.

"One to wear an' one to sit on," said George in answer to Wheatley's questioning look. Pointing to the dark sky over the Downs, the blacksmith continued, "Be pouring cats'n'dogs afor we'm halfway there." So saying he pulled a sack around his shoulders, climbed into the trap, placed a piece of sacking on the transverse bench nearest to the front and sat on it. Wheatley similarly placed one of his sacks on the bench opposite to the blacksmith before he sat down, but put the other next to him. The blacksmith looked pointedly at the sack. Wheatley looked pointedly at the sky where a weak sun was peeking through the clouds, the drizzle having stopped for the first time that day. Shrugging, George picked up the reins, performed a double tongue-click and the flimsy conveyance lurched into motion.

Within ten minutes the sun had disappeared, the heavens had opened and Wheatley was soaked before he had a chance to pull his sack around his shoulders. As far as he could tell all the sacking did was mop up water like a sponge, though the driver seemed to bear the discomfort stoically. Indeed, the worsening weather seemed to loosen his tongue.

"You'm visitin' Mrs Stephens then?"

"Yes," said Wheatley, who did not wish to reveal the reason for his journey and besides, was in no mood for conversation with rain dripping from his hat brim and finding its way beneath his collar.

George waited a few minutes.

"You'm a relative or something like that?"

"No," said Wheatley.

George was obviously not going to take the hint, "Tragic life, the Widow Stephens," he tried. When there was no reply he continued, "First her daughter, then her husband. Gone." When this also elicited no response he said, "Well He giveth an' He taketh away, I s'pose. Damn shame, though"

Wheatley realised that his driver had just confirmed the main reason for his journey. The daughter of the house was indeed deceased as Miss Yardley had said. Obviously a different Millie Stephens. He was damply wondering whether he need continue further when with a "Whoa there," George halted the conveyance. Exiting the trap, he pulled open a gate in the hedge, did a double click with his tongue before saying, "Walk on!" To Wheatley's great surprise, the pony pulled the trap through the gateway and then halted to wait for its master. George closed the gate, got back in opposite Wheatley and they set off again along a rough track.

"Used to be a proper good'un this farm one time," said George. "Gone a bit to seed since Farmer Stephens went before."

The track was short and they entered an enclosed farmyard through a gap between a stable and what Wheatley took to be a pig sty. The detective was a townie but even he could see that the area was run down. The farmhouse, a solid two-storey affair with flint walls and a thatched roof, was to their left with several battered-looking outbuildings to their right. Directly ahead of them was a barn, its double doors wide open, one drooping on a single hinge. George drove the pony and trap directly into the barn.

"Should keep the rain orf while we wait," he said. "I'll be here when you want to go back."

"Thank you," said Wheatley, deciding that as he had arrived, he might as well carry on with his planned interview. Dismounting and doubtfully eyeing a large hole in the roof through which the rain was pouring, he saw that the blacksmith had removed a nose-bag from beneath his seat and the pony was now munching contentedly. As Wheatley left the barn, George was fully occupied drying off his steed with the piece of sacking the detective had been sitting on.

The only creatures Wheatley saw as he tried to avoid the mud on his way to the farmhouse were a few chickens pecking desultorily at the ground. Thankfully there was a porch sheltering the farmhouse door, as the detective's first knock yielded nothing. Using his fist to knock louder, he was rewarded by the sounds of unlocking and the door opening.

"Can I help you?"

The woman was grey-haired and slightly stooped with age. Her slim figure and quality clothing belied the image Wheatley had of a typical farmer's wife. In his mind, country wives were rotund and jolly. They wore rough clothing and were always wiping their hands on an apron. He had no time to extend this image as the woman said, "Good Heavens, you're soaked. Come in, come in. You been standing there long? People usually come round the back." With no answer seemingly expected, he found himself being ushered into a warm kitchen. The woman took his hat and insisted he remove his overcoat and jacket which were wet through. Placing a shawl around his shoulders, she established him in a chair in front of the range where he sat, his trousers steaming, while she prepared a pot of tea.

Wheatley had decamped to the kitchen table and sat nursing a cup of strong tea while his coat and jacket hung, drying, in front of the fire by the time the woman, who had introduced herself as Mrs Stephens, returned from taking a hot drink to George in the barn. A waft of cold, damp air presaged her arrival. Removing an old oil-skin she had used to shelter herself as she crossed the farmyard and hanging it on a hook on the kitchen door, she settled herself at the table with Wheatley.

"Now, what can I do for you, Mr Wheatley?"

"It concerned your daughter, Mrs Stephens. I believe she was called Millicent and was employed in service in Brighton."

Mrs Stephens slumped in her chair. She raised her hand to tremble across her cheek. Her face had changed from friendly inquisitiveness to abject sadness in an instant and Wheatley wondered briefly if he had been a little blunt and was about to say that it was almost certainly a different Millie Stephens he was interested in when the woman began to speak.

"It's silly, I know. Ten years past and I still miss her terribly. When she was working away, I thought of her always and counted the days to her next visit. I still think of her every day now, but she'll never visit again."

On the words 'visit again', the distraught woman's voice cracked and she turned away, showing her heaving back to the detective. Wheatley wondered what he should do. He had not expected such a reaction. At one point he hesitantly moved his hand towards the woman wondering if he should offer some physical comfort, but he rethought and withdrew the hand. In the end he did nothing. Slowly the shaking subsided and Mrs Stephens turned back towards him.

"Sorry, detective." She gave a sharp intake of breath, then continued. "I know you're here to do your job but what do the police want with a poor girl dead these ten years? What do you want to know about my Millie?"

Wheatley knew he was in over his head. He had come on the off chance that Miss Yardley at the letting agency had got it wrong. That she had mixed Millie up with another girl. That *his* Millicent Stephens was this poor woman's daughter. But now he had caused all sorts of upset when in fact George the blacksmith had already confirmed that the daughter could not be the Millicent Stephens Wheatley was interested in. Should he apologise? Could he make up a more plausible reason for his visit, say it wasn't about Millie really? Should he just leave?

Fortunately, he was relieved from making a decision by Mrs Stephens continuing.

"It killed my John, you know," she said almost to herself.

"John?" said Wheatley.

"My husband." Wheatley remembered George referring to the 'Widow Stephens'. Remembered too late to prevent more tears, he supposed, but was surprised when Mrs Stephens continued almost matter of factly, "He could never get over it. Always fretting about why it happened. Never relaxing to mourn her properly. And the anger in him."

"He was violent?" asked Wheatley.

"Not John, no. He was the gentlest of men. To me and the girls anyway." She smiled and nodded her head slowly. "He was just so angry at how it happened."

"Was foul play expected?" said Wheatley, confident now on the familiar ground of police business.

It was as if an iron curtain had descended. Mrs Stephens raised herself from her slump, and her face stony, said, "Nothing like that. He's dead. She's dead. Nothing more to say on the matter. Now is there anything else before you go on your way?"

Wheatley wasn't sure what he had done wrong, but he didn't want to leave before he had at least tried to put it right.

"So you have to work the farm yourself?" he said. He didn't know why. It was the first thing that came into his mind and he cursed himself for not being able to say something more soothing. For not being able to think of the right thing. But amazingly it did the trick. Mrs Stephens visibly relaxed and it was her that made the peace.

"Don't mind me," she said. "It's just that it all comes flooding back."

She paused at this and Wheatley wondered whether to say something more, but the widow continued, "Me? Work the farm? Bless you, no." She went on to explain that she let the fields to a neighbouring farmer, retaining just the actual farmyard for herself.

"I have my vegetable garden, a few fruit bushes and my chickens," she said. "I'll get a weaner soon, fatten him up over the summer and slaughter in the autumn. Gives enough bacon and salt pork to last me the winter. I does well enough."

Wheatley noticed that as she entered a happier state of mind, she began to develop more of the Sussex twang in her voice.

"Another cup of tea, Mr Wheatley?"

"No, thank you, Mrs Stephens, I've taken enough of your time," said Wheatley, relieved that the awkwardness he had caused previously now seemed to have dissipated. He moved to retrieve his jacket and coat from in front of the kitchen range. As he shrugged into his jacket, noting that it was still damp but pleasingly warm, he observed an ornately framed photograph stood in the centre of the mantel above the range. The picture showed a younger, but unmistakeable Mrs Stephens sitting on a bench next to a pretty girl in her late teens or early twenties. Leaning over them was a burly man in what were his best clothes judging by the stiffness of his collar. He had one hand on Mrs Stephens' shoulder, the other gripped his pipe. Sitting cross legged on the floor at Mrs Stephens' feet was a young girl, her face somewhat blurred.

"That's my John," said Mrs Stephens, leaning past Wheatley and picking up the photograph. "That's still my best dress," she mused, before returning the photograph to the mantel. "That's Millie," she continued, pointing to the girl sharing the bench. Though similar in build, and from what he could see from the monochrome photograph, in colouring, it was not the Millicent Stephens Wheatley knew. Further confirmation that he had had a wasted journey.

"That photograph was taken the year before it happened." Mrs Stephens sighed and Wheatley began to feel uncomfortable again. Thankfully she quickly rallied. Smiling, she said, "That Susan could never sit still."

"Who is Susan?" Wheatley asked.

"Our youngest. Susan. There." She pointed to the girl sitting on the floor. "She was eight years old then. Moved her head while the photographer was counting. We couldn't afford another, so there she is, all blurred."

Wheatley looked carefully at the family photograph. "I think perhaps I would like another cup of tea after all," he said. "If you don't mind."

"No bother at all," said Mrs Stephens, "I'll top up the pot."

After the refreshing of the pot of tea, it wasn't difficult to get Mrs Stephens to talk about her youngest daughter. "Is she in service too?" asked Wheatley after her mother had confirmed that she worked away.

"At first she wanted to be a nurse. I blame my John for that, always telling the girls stories when they were young. And the one our Susan always wanted was about Florence Nightingale, the Lady with the Lamp. Caught her imagination somehow." Mrs Stephens smiled at this and Wheatley progressed the conversation by asking whether her daughter was still nursing.

"No, she soon gave that up. I think it was very different from the stories. She said if she had wanted to spend her life skivvying, she'd have followed Millie into service. But of course after what happened to Millie, she wouldn't dream of it. Now she works in one of those posh shops in London. You know, the ones that sell everything?"

Wheatley was still unsure what exactly had happened to Millie, but as neither of the Stephens daughters seemed to have anything to do with his case, he decided not to chance upsetting the widow again. "Department stores," he said automatically.

"That's it, department stores. I've a picture somewhere."

She went to the dresser and pulled out one drawer, then another, finally saying, "Here it is."

She came back to sit at the table and handed Wheatley a well-thumbed postcard. On the front a small number of men in suits were surrounded by a large number of girls and women, all dressed identically in long black skirts and high-necked white blouses with leg of mutton sleeves. They were standing outside of a corner shopfront. The words 'Messrs Swan and Edgar of Piccadilly, Purveyors of Fine Merchandise' had been superimposed in a scroll on the picture.

"My Susan's at the back, there," said Mrs Stephens. "She put a ring round her head because it's difficult to tell who's who."

Wheatley looked closely at the girl with the pencil ring around her head, but in reality, the photograph had been taken from so far away that she could have been anybody. On the back of the card was written, 'Mrs J Stephens, Meadow Farm, Hassocks, Sussex', while adjacent to the address a well-formed hand had written:

8th April 1893
    Dear Ma,
    This is a picture of me and the girls in front of the store. I've put a ring round my head because it was to advertise the shop really and the faces have not come out

very clear. I hope you are well. I can't wait until next
month when I shall see you again.

From your loving and obedient daughter,
Susan

"She mentions seeing you in May?" said Wheatley as he returned the postcard.

"My birthday," Mrs Stephens said. "She's a good girl my Susan, always comes to see me without fail every Mothering Sunday, on my birthday and at Christmas."

"She sounds very dutiful," said Wheatley.

"Yes, never misses. She was late last year, mind. For my birthday. Something wrong with the trains, she said. But she got here."

"Which day was that?" Wheatley asked.

"I told you. My birthday. Seventeenth of May."

"So you did," said Wheatley. "Well, thank you for the tea, Mrs Stephens, and for the drying. I am so sorry to have bothered you. I'll be going now."

"No bother at all, Mr Wheatley, and sorry for my silliness. In some ways it has been good to talk about it. Now, it's coming down like stair rods out there." She reached to the hook on the back of the kitchen door and took down her oil-skin. "Put this over you, otherwise all that drying will have gone to waste. Leave it with old George. He'll drop it in next time he's passing."

The journey back was spent mostly in silence. As they passed through Keymer, George pointed out the church of St Cosmas and St Damian.

"Widow Stephen's daughter's buried there," he said.

"Interesting name," said Wheatley. "I thought I knew most of the blessed saints, but I haven't heard of those two."

George obviously had nothing to say to that. He lapsed back into silence and the journey continued in that way; Wheatley fretting about his wasted time, George considering whatever blacksmiths think about on cold, wet days in a pony and trap.

As they approached the railway station, George said, "You'm a copper, then?"

"Detective Wheatley, Brighton Municipal Constabulary." Wheatley saw no point in prevaricating now he was on his way back. "How did you know?"

"Couldn't be anything else with them boots," said the blacksmith, nodding towards Wheatley's feet. "Besides, Widow Stephens told me when she brought me a cuppa," he said a minute or so later.

The pony and trap continued on its way. Wheatley, suddenly taking an interest in their progress, cleared his throat and mentioned to his driver that they were passing the station by.

"Not taking you to the station. Taking you to the Friar's Oak."

"The Friar's Oak? What's that?"

"Pub," said George.

"No, thank you for the thought but I don't need a public house, I need to get the train back to Brighton."

"Fanny Bunting works at the Friar's Oak."

"Fanny Bunting?"

"You need to talk to her."

"Why do I need to talk to her?"

"Because Fanny Bunting were Millie Stephen's best friend," the blacksmith said forcefully. "And because there'm more than one body in that grave back there."

*

"I don't talk to coppers," hissed Fanny Bunting, then louder, "what can I get for you?"

Wheatley had been parked at the far end of the public bar of the Friar's Oak while a woman behind the counter he took to be Miss Bunting had a whispered but obvious argument with Old George the Blacksmith. Eventually George had gone to sit on a bench under the window and the woman had flounced over to where Wheatley was standing. Now this. It really was the last straw! Keeping his voice low, he said, "Very well. You don't talk to coppers. I don't want a drink. In truth, I don't understand why I am here. So, unless you can keep a civil tongue in your head, I'm leaving to catch my train."

Fanny still looked angry but she visibly pulled herself together, even managed a gritted smile.

"That's very kind of you, sir. I'll be right back," she said loudly before turning and walking to the beer pumps. When Fanny returned, she plonked two glasses of beer on the counter before them.

"Pint and a half of mild. That'll be thruppence farthing."

Wheatley looked down at the drinks he hadn't ordered, much of which had been spilled by their none too gentle landing, then up at Fanny's outstretched hand.

"The extra farthing's for my half. Two halves cost a ha'penny more than a pint," she explained as if that was the reason for Wheatley's hesitation. The stand-off lasted for less than a minute before Wheatley groped in his pocket and pulled out a florin, the first coin he found.

"I hope you don't expect any change for that," said Fanny, pocketing the coin. "Now, Old George tells me you are asking about poor Millie."

The detective began to say 'I thought you don't speak to coppers', thought better of it and replied, "I was, but it appears she isn't the Millicent Stephens I am interested in."

"Well, she ought to be." Fanny Bunting seemed to be getting even angrier, something Wheatley would have considered impossible. "You ought to have done something ten years ago." To Wheatley's discomfort, the barmaid's anger dissipated into tears. "It's criminal what that man did to her, made her do. And your lot did nothing."

Fanny was now sobbing and Wheatley realised that they were becoming the centre of attention, the buzz of conversation in the bar almost silenced. He considered his options. What he wanted to do was run. To leave the public house and get on a train back to Brighton as quickly as possible. Instead he found himself saying, "Miss Bunting, is there somewhere quiet we can go to discuss this more privately?"

Fanny Bunting's sleeves were rolled up and she used the full length of her bare forearm to draw across her face as she took in a long liquid breath through her nose. Then she turned and walked over to a large man standing smoking a pipe, one elbow propped on the shelf above the bar's open fire. They had a brief, whispered conversation. The man nodded, tapped out his pipe on the grate and went and stood behind the bar.

"Follow me," said Fanny, opening an internal glass door. "Bring the drinks."

"There's never anyone in here this time of day," said Fanny. The door led into the saloon bar where the walls were panelled and the floor polished rather than the whitewash and sawdust of the public bar. "Sorry about that back there," she continued. "I just get so angry. It was such a waste.'

"Perhaps you could tell me what happened," said Wheatley.

"It all started when I worked for the Regency Letting Agency in Brighton…"

Fanny went on to tell how she and Millie Stephens were best friends. Fanny went to work as a ladies' maid in Brighton, and when there was a vacancy, she recommended Millie.

"That was in the old days when Mr Owens owned the business. Proper swank it was then. Every house had a tweeney and a ladies' maid as well as a cook and footman. We both worked in houses in the best areas." Wheatley asked whether she remembered 28, Grand Parade, but she didn't, having worked mainly on Kings' Road.

"It was only for the Season, of course, we were back each year in time for the harvest. We had a lovely time together in Brighton, though. Miss Yardley made sure we had the same day off each fortnight. But then Millie met *him,* and everything changed."

Fanny explained how after they had been working together for some five years a single gentleman had taken the house Millie was due to work in.

"She expected to be told she wasn't wanted, but the gentleman said as he hadn't brought his valet with him, would she fill in as it were. Not helping him dress, nothing sordid like that. But laying out clothes and brushing and hanging those he'd worn. Sounded a doddle to Millie so she said yes. I suppose that's how it started."

The barmaid went on to explain how gradually Millie stopped seeing her every other Thursday. 'Always some excuse or another.' Then the day came when she found out what was really happening.

"She admitted it to me one of the few days we spent together that last summer. She was in love, the silly cow. Said they was running away together to get married when his inheritance came through. When was that I asked? Soon, she said, on his thirtieth birthday. I told her! 'He's just having fun,' I said. Toffs like him don't marry girls like us. But she wasn't having none of it. 'You be careful my girl,' I said. But of course, she wasn't."

Fanny picked up her glass and impressively drank it all in one draught.

"I saw him once," she said. "It was Millie's sister's ninth birthday and she'd arranged for Susan to come down for the day. We were all going to celebrate together." She went on to describe how John Stephens had taken Susan to Hassocks station and put her on a train and Fanny and Millie had met her at Brighton.

"She was so excited. She idolised her big sister. Anyway, we went down to the sea-front and had just bought Susan an ice-cream from the hokey-pokey man when Millie goes all giggly and calls out, 'Cecil, over here'. Over comes this man dressed in one of those stripey blazers all the toffs wear, doffing his straw boater and slobbering over Millie's outstretched hand."

Here Fanny made a moue and shuddered.

"Tried that with me too but I was having none of it. Susan watched wide eyed as he put his hat back on, said 'A pleasure, ladies,' and left rapidly, swinging that silver topped cane of his."

"Can you remember what he looked like?" Wheatley asked.

"Well, he already looked nearer forty to me," said Fanny. "Short bloke, running a bit to fat. Don't know what she saw in him. But she was besotted. Never did tell me his name neither."

"But she called him Cecil?" said Wheatley.

"Something like that, does it matter?"

Wheatley thought that it possibly did matter. That perhaps his visit had not been a complete waste of time after all.

"I assume it didn't end well," he said.

Fanny picked up Wheatley's untouched drink, filled her empty glass from it and swallowed at least half before continuing.

"No, it bloody didn't."

The story Fanny told was a tragic but all too familiar one. Finding out that Millie was with child, her beau was far from forthright in fulfilling his marriage promises.

"He took her to one of the last bits of Pimlico still standing. You know what hovels they were," said Fanny. While he was aware of the area Fanny was talking about, the last of Brighton's notorious slums had been cleared while he was still a boy. But all the same he nodded in encouragement.

"He stood on the doorstep, handed over a few coins to some old crone, pushed Millie through the door of the rathole and left, never to be seen again. She hardly knew what was happening, poor girl, and when she was chucked out onto the street, bleeding and in pain, she didn't know what to do. So she came to me."

Fanny Bunting paused for breath. She looked drained, sitting with her head bowed, her hands on the table either side of her empty glass, trembling. Wheatley felt helpless. The woman so obviously distraught dragging up the past. He wondered if there was anything he could do.

"Is there anything I can do?" he asked.

"Gin," said Fanny. "Large."

Wheatley went to the bar twice, the first large gin disappearing as soon as he had set it down.

"Funny, I don't seem to have any tears left," said Fanny in a quiet voice before continuing with her tale. Millie had come to the house where Fanny was working, banging on the door and waking the whole household. "She was hardly able to walk but the sod who was renting the house told me to get rid of her, and quick." So, Fanny and she had talked in one of the seafront shelters nearby.

"'You need to go to hospital, my girl,' I said, once she'd told me everything, but she was having none of it. 'I can't. I'll be arrested. I can't go to gaol,' she said. 'All I want is to go home. I want my mum!' Well, she wasn't bleeding too badly then so I sneaked back into the house to get some towels for padding. You know, for 'down there'." Fanny pointed below the table with both her index fingers. "Then somehow I got her up to the station. We had a bit of a wait, but the milk train came in around five and we got that back up."

Fanny was now talking at quite a pace. Explaining how, when they arrived at Hassocks, she had left Millie in the waiting room while she went and knocked up George the blacksmith to harness his pony and trap. How when they got to Meadow Farm, George had gone on to Ditchling for the doctor while Millie had been rushed to bed. About the confusion and the anger and the blood.

"It was a little girl," said Fanny. "Stillborn, of course. Millie had lost consciousness, died soon after. Never even saw her daughter. We put the poor thing in the coffin with her mother. Doctor said there was nothing he could have done. But he was kind. Put 'influenza' on the death certificate."

There was more. About how the whole thing was hushed up so as not to bring shame on the family. How John Stephens had taken to drink in his anguish and died in an accident while drunk. How Mrs Stephens had devoted her time to Susan until Susan also left. Eventually Fanny's words matched her tears and dried up. Wheatley and Fanny sat in silence for some time after that. Then Wheatley had asked whether the death had been reported to the police.

"They didn't want to know," said Fanny. "Sussex Police said that it was Brighton's problem as the offence had taken place in Brighton. Brighton Constabulary said the death was in Sussex, so it was their case. In the end nobody did nothing."

Wheatley had said he was sorry. Fanny just nodded. He then showed her the photograph of Charlie Runcorn taken at the autopsy, asking if this was Millie's Cecil.

"It could be," she'd said, "but it could be anyone. I only saw him once and it was a long time ago."

This time it was Fanny who said she was sorry, and Wheatley who did the nodding. So, they sat again in silence until George the blacksmith entered and gently steered Fanny back into the bar. "We'll take care of her now," he said.

"So now you know," George said later while driving the detective to the railway station and Wheatley agreed that he did, though he was unsure what he could do with the information.

"As long as you know," said George. "It's important somebody official knows the truth of it."

*

Wheatley sat on the train trying to decide whether he had made any progress in his enquiries. He had a girl with the same name as a girl in his case who had been severely wronged by a man who might or might not be one of his murder victims. He had a devoted sister of the wronged girl who would now be the same age as his Millie Stephens but who couldn't be her because Susan Stephens lived and worked in London. The only connection with his case seemed to be the Regency Letting Agency and he resolved to pay them another visit. He also had the mystery of the Garsons, who had vanished. Unless of course they didn't live in Kent after all. Then there was the mystery woman, the other murder victim. And the girl who had disappeared. In all it seemed the case had become even more complicated. He decided to sleep on it. But first he would return to the Detective Office and send a telegram to Detective Winstanley of the Metropolitan Police.

Wednesday 21st February 1894

The long climb to the Offices of the Regency Letting
Agency once again left Wheatley breathless. After a pause
he gave a quick knock on the door and entered the cramped
office.

"Can I help you?" Miss Yardley asked, rising to her
feet. "Oh, it's you, Detective Wheatley," she said sinking
back into her chair. "I'm afraid Mr Coughlin is unavailable
today."

"Actually, it is you I have come to see, Miss Yardley,"
said the detective, "Just a few enquiries."

Wheatley reminded the receptionist of their previous
conversation about Millicent Stephens and asked whether
her younger sister had ever been employed by the agency.

"I knew she had a sister but wasn't she much younger?
An infant, I thought."

"I was thinking more recently, say in the last year?"
said Wheatley.

"No, certainly not," said Miss Yardley. "We don't
employ maids any more, not since Mr Coughlin took
over."

Wheatley showed her the mortuary picture of Charlie
Runcorn and asked if she could confirm that he was the
gentlemen who rented number 28, Grand Parade, but she

couldn't, saying that almost all Seasonal lettings were arranged by letter.

"Would you have the letter by any chance?" asked Wheatley.

Miss Yardley confirmed that she had and retrieved a folder from the filing cabinet on her right. She opened the file and passed a letter to the detective. It was on quality paper, Wheatley noted. It was signed 'Sir Tobias Hughes-Lewthwaite, baronet,' but the return address was a hotel in South London, not the Marylebone address where the real Tobias Hughes-Lewthwaite lived.

"Do you still have files from when Millicent Stephens worked for you?" he said on the off-chance.

The receptionist did. This time she needed to move around the office and she and the detective performed a pas-de-deux in the restricted space so that she could reach into the bottom of a cupboard set into the wall. There was a definite smell of damp as she opened it and Wheatley hoped that any paperwork was still readable.

"It's the last place that Millie worked that I'm interested in."

After yet more juxtapositioning, Miss Yardley returned to her seat with several faded-looking folders which she proceeded to leaf through.

"Yes, here we are," she said, "It was 3, King's Road, reserved by a Mr Cecil de Vere."

For the first time, Wheatley felt that perhaps he was beginning to get somewhere in this case.

"Was this Mr de Vere a regular client?" he asked.

"Certainly not," said Miss Yardley, "There's a very clear instruction in the file never to let to him again. His cheque was not honoured, you see. He still owes us a Season's rent."

"I don't suppose you have his letter of reservation?"

Miss Yardley did and she passed it to the detective. Wheatley placed it next to the letter from 'Sir Tobias Hughes-Lewthwaite'. To his eye, the handwriting seemed identical. He decided that later he would ask Pettit his opinion as an artist.

"I need to take these letters with me as evidence," he said.

"I shall require a receipt," said the receptionist.

*

It's all climbing today, thought Wheatley to himself as he reached the top of Trafalgar Street and stood in front of Brighton Railway Station. The trip to Shoreham was probably a wild goose chase anyway, as Millie had said the Garsons lived in Kent. When he bought a ticket and was informed that strictly speaking the town was called New Shoreham, he was even more convinced that he was wasting his time.

Exiting New Shoreham Station, Wheatley could see a prominent church tower which had a strange contraption on top of it resembling a spike impaling a ball. Assuming that the town would be clustered around the church, he headed towards it. The church was called St Mary de

Haura, another name Wheatley hadn't heard before. A helpful passer-by informed him that 'de Haura' was old English for 'of the harbour' and that the tower was clearly visible from the sea. The ball on top ascended and descended with the tide, informing ships when it was safe to enter the harbour, which dried at low tide. Fascinated as he was by this, Wheatley was anxious to get back to work and asked if there was a street called New Road in Shoreham. His voluble companion confirmed that there was and proceeded to give directions.

"Keep going towards the river, turn left at the school and past the old Town Hall," he said, before bidding Wheatley good day.

New Road was easy to find. On one side was a yard which housed a haulage company and a smithy. Opposite and next to the school was a good-sized building which Wheatley took to be the old Town Hall. After this the road opened out to fields on his left. The buildings on his right also soon gave way to uninterrupted views over the river, and beyond to the sea. None of them were private residences and the road became more of a track the further from the town centre Wheatley went. He was minded to turn round having decided he was on a wasted journey but seeing there was another cluster of buildings at the far end of the road, he resolved to leave no stone unturned. Where New Road met the Coast Road there were a few tumble-down cottages. There were no numbers, no names visible, so Wheatley knocked at the first. His knock was unanswered, even though he could swear there was a rustling from within. The next dwelling had a rough curtain instead of a door with a bell hanging next to where the door should be. Wheatley tried to ring the bell, but discovered it had no clapper. He was staring confusedly into the body of the bell when the curtain was pulled back and a person said, "What do you want?" When there was no reply, "Well, I haven't got all day. I said, what do you want?" followed rapidly.

Wheatley had been staring. He knew he had. The person who answered was short, very weighty and smoking a clay pipe. They were almost bald with a hint of a moustache but wearing a threadbare woman's dress stretched over a large belly and small breasts, the dress riding up to reveal a pair of fisherman's boots. Wheatley was trying to decide how to address this person when they turned impatiently away from him.

"Er, I'm looking for a Mr and Mrs Garson, I believe they live in New Road," Wheatley said hurriedly.

The person turned back, took the pipe from their mouth and let out an earthy laugh.

"Mr and Mrs Garson, is it? Well, Micah Garson and his fat trollop live two doors up that way when they can bother to be here."

And with that, they disappeared back through the curtain into the house.

*

"I don't know where she got Kent from," said Micah Garson. "My family have lived here since my Great Grandfather came here in the time of the Prince Regent. Silly place to settle, really, what with the war and the Frenchies just over the water. Still, that was over in my grandfather's time, and after that…"

"Detective's not here to listen to you going on about your family," interrupted Mrs Garson. "Don't encourage him, sir, or he'll go on and on."

Wheatley, who had no intention of encouraging the footman, was seated on a bench under the window of the single beaten-earth floored room that formed the ground floor of the Garsons' cottage. The rear wall opposite was taken up by an open chimney containing a kitchen range where Mrs Garson stood waiting for the kettle to boil before preparing a pot of tea. Micah Garson occupied a wooden armchair pulled close to one side of the range while an empty rocker on the other side awaited Mrs Garson's ample frame.

"Did you work with Millie very often?" asked the detective.

"Never seen her before," said the subdued Mr Garson.

"We was surprised when she turned up," said Mrs Garson, handing Wheatley a cup of strong, black tea. "Haven't had maids supplied since Mr Owens' demise."

"But she was employed by the agency?"

"So she said," said Micah.

"We thought the gentleman might have brought her, but she said Miss Yardley sent her," added Mrs Garson.

"Did either of you check?" asked Wheatley.

"Why would we do that? Another pair of hands is another pair of hands," said Micah.

"Once we welcomes the guests, we is generally left alone," said Mrs Garson.

"And that's the way we like it!" said Micah Garson, pouring his tea into his saucer and blowing noisily to cool it.

"We assumed with Miss Stephanie in residence, Sir Tobias had paid extra for a ladies' maid," said Mrs Garson, subsiding into her chair and impressively holding her cup at arm's length so that the rocking did not cause her tea to spill over her.

"Not that he paid for anything, extra or no, from what I hear," said Micah. "We certainly didn't get our customary tips this year."

"Speaking of Sir Tobias and Miss Stephanie," said Wheatley, moving the conversation on so as not to provoke a rant from Micah Garson about money. He removed the post-mortem photographs of Charlie Runcorn and the mystery murder victim from his pocket, along with Pettit's sketch of Miss Stephanie. "Can you confirm these likenesses?"

Wheatley placed the drawing and photographs on the dirt floor at his feet, oriented towards the Garsons. Mr and Mrs Garson leant forwards in their chairs, then both nodded and sat back at the same time.

"That's them," said Micah Garson.

Picking up the photograph of the mystery murder victim, Wheatley said, "I don't suppose either of you recognise this woman."

The Garsons frowned at each other.

"We told you," said Micah.

"Miss Stephanie," said Mrs Garson.

Wheatley assumed that the couple had become confused. He picked up Pettit's drawing and held it out towards them. "This is Miss Stephanie," he said.

Mrs Garson took the drawing, looked at it for a few seconds, then held it out towards her husband. He lent forward, shrugged his shoulders and sat back into his armchair. Mrs Garson turned it towards herself once more, gave it a few more seconds perusal, then handed it back to the detective.

"I don't know who this woman is," she said. "But that photograph there, that's Miss Stephanie what disappeared from the house we was working in. I'd stake me life on it."

"Mine too," affirmed Micah Garson.

Thursday 22nd February 1894.

Wheatley sat in the Detective Office with the Hughes-Lewthwaite file open in front of him.

"Shouldn't you be going? Your shift ended over an hour ago," said Edwards who had just returned after investigating a break-in in one of the shops on Western Road.

"The Inspector said to wait to report to him about this case," Wheatley said, indicating the file. "Though what I'll say with so much conflicting evidence, I've no idea."

"All comes down to who you believe, I'd say," said Edwards, hanging his hat and coat and then indicating that Wheatley should vacate the desk.

"How do you mean?" Wheatley hastily shuffled the flimsy carbon copies of his report together, the originals already in the hands of Inspector Cronin.

"Well, Miss Millicent says one thing, the Garsons another. Who's most likely to be telling the truth?"

"Or perhaps one of them is merely mistaken," said Wheatley, standing and placing his file on a shelf behind the one desk of the Detective Office.

"Makes no difference really," said Edwards, seating himself. "I assume you checked where the Garsons were when the second body was found."

"Of course. They say they were in Shoreham. Provided many names of people who might have seen them out and about. Several of them confirmed that they were in the town on that day. But of course, it's less than half an hour by train from New Shoreham to Brighton and all were rather hazy about the specific time they saw Mr or Mrs Garson."

Edwards appeared about to continue the conversation when there was a cursory knock and Sergeant Johnson put his head around the Detective Office door.

"Inspector's calling for you, Wheatley," he stated before moving away, leaving the door ajar.

"Better not keep his nibs waiting," said Edwards.

Inspector Cronin was once again seated at his desk rather than the armchair by the fire when Wheatley entered the office. What is more, he seemed to have been working. The normally pristine desk was covered with papers which the Inspector was arranging into some sort of order.

"About time to put this case to bed, eh Whatley?" he said.

"Well sir, there are still complications which have to be resolved." *Not least the 'complication' of not knowing who the murderer is*, thought Wheatley.

"Yes, I see that you have been gallivanting all over Sussex for unlikely reasons. Might one take it as read that you liaised correctly with the Sussex Constabularies? We would not like a repeat of the debacle you caused with the Metropolitan Police Force, would we?"

Wheatley felt a heat rise in his chest, surround his neck and flood his face. Of course he should have consulted the West Sussex Constabulary. But that would have taken time. Too much time. And besides, he hadn't thought of it and now the embarrassment of repeating so basic a mistake was showing in his face, which he felt sure was glowing red. Fortunately there seemed to be no need to answer.

"Very well, Whatley, we'll take that as read, then." Wheatley could swear that there was a smile on the Inspector's face as he looked up and said, "Now tell me about these complications."

Wheatley repeated his findings about the Regency Letting Agency and its claim that it did not provide maids, the Millie Stephens mystery and the confusion about whether the drawing or the post-mortem photograph showed the missing 'Miss Stephanie', all of which he knew was in the file in front of the Inspector.

"Surely you are complicating this too much," said Inspector Cronin. "This…" Here he paused to consult the file. "This Charlie Runcorn, alias Cecil de Vere, alias Sir Tobias Hughes-Lewthwaite, this well-known trickster, has a contretemps with his lady friend, kills her in an act of passion and later is killed by person or persons unknown who have certainly fled the vicinity. Probably one of the people he inveigled into lending him money."

"On that track, sir," said Wheatley, seizing the opportunity, "did the enquiries at your Masonic Lodge yield any possible leads?"

It was as if he hadn't spoken. The Inspector merely continued, "So there we have it. The disappearance and the first murder solved. The second murderer unlikely to be found."

"But the necroscopy indicated the same murderer for both victims."

"A conclusion drawn by a lady doctor with little experience of murder and the heightened imagination of her sex."

Wheatley was determined to ride over such objections. He continued, "We also don't know for certain that the murdered woman on the beach was the missing Miss Stephanie. Miss Stephens and the Garsons tell different stories."

"Servants, Detective, completely unreliable. Surely it's simpler if the missing girl and the murdered woman are one and the same?"

"Simpler, but not necessarily true," said Wheatley, trying to hide his increasing annoyance. "Plus the Regency Agency denying they employed maids."

"As I said, servants are unreliable witnesses. The girl just got confused. Probably employed directly by the lessor. And as for the two Millicent Stephens, pure coincidence. Neither Millicent nor Stephens are exactly uncommon names."

"But sir…"

"But nothing, Constable. I can see this case is taking its toll on you. Surely you can see that it would be better to conclude as I have suggested."

"In all conscience I could not do that, sir," said Wheatley, clenching his fists by his side in an attempt to remain professional and keep the emotions he was feeling from showing in his voice.

"You are not going to let this lie are you, Wheatley?" said the Inspector.

"No, sir, I am not!" said Wheatley. Professionalism vanquished, he spun to storm out of the door. The voice that halted him was not one he had heard issue from the Inspector before. Clipped and commanding, giving an order one did not ignore.

"I did not give permission for you to leave, Detective Constable Wheatley. Resume your position immediately"

An order which Wheatley obeyed unthinkingly, turning back to stand at attention in front of the Inspector's desk.

"Wait here," said the Inspector, shuffling the papers from the desk into their folder. He placed the folder under his arm and walked past the Detective. Wheatley heard the door open and muffled voices before the door was closed again. When he turned, a stranger was walking towards him — a tall, lean, well-dressed man with a full head of salt and pepper hair and a nattily clipped moustache, his gait suggesting he favoured his left leg. He held out his hand in greeting.

"Gray. Colonel. Retired," he said.

Wheatley noticed that the Colonel's handshake was rather soft and so, remembering Detective Winstanley's lesson, used his thumb to press between the joints on

Colonel Gray's index finger. He had to concentrate and look at the clasped hands to do this, and as he raised his eyes afterwards, the Colonel was smiling at him. He felt his hand gripped at the wrist and held gently but firmly by Colonel Gray who removed his right hand from Wheatley's and still smiling said, "Not bad, young man, but it's more than a handshake that identifies a true follower of the craft." Taking no notice of Wheatley's embarrassment, Colonel Gray added, "Shouldn't try that too often, by the way. Another fellow might take offence at what could be called impersonation." He then released Wheatley and made his way to the fireside where he sat himself comfortably in one of the Inspector's armchairs. "Won't you join me?" he asked, taking up the poker from the companion set in the hearth and stirring the already healthy fire into further life. "Fellows who spend one's youth in warmer climes find it rather chilly this time of year," he offered as way of explanation.

At any time of year if the Inspector is anything to go by, thought Wheatley, sitting rigidly on the chair.

"Didn't take the easy way out then?" said the Colonel when they were settled.

"Sir?" said Wheatley, who was bemused by the Inspector's disappearance and replacement by this military man.

"Cronin said you wouldn't. But he said he'd offer it anyway in case he was mistaken."

"Mistaken?" Wheatley was aware that his contribution to the conversation was mere parroting, but he was having trouble making sense of its direction.

"About you. 'Wheatley will want to see it through'," he said. "'He's the type who wants every 't' crossed and every 'i' dotted, bit like old Carstairs'."

"Carstairs?"

"Major Carstairs, adjutant of the regiment when Cronin joined. A very thorough man. Why I'm here, you see? I'm the reserve position."

Wheatley decided it was time to pull himself together and act like a policeman rather than a confused schoolboy. "No. Sir, I don't see. And frankly I'm as amazed that the Inspector knows my name as the fact that you suggest that he might approve of my actions."

"Used the old 'no idea who you are' routine, did he? What did he call you? Wheelie? No, Waitly? Not Watson?"

"Whatley, usually," said Wheatley.

"Classic, keep a fella on his toes, what? Splendid chap, Cronin. He was a subaltern to my captain in Egypt. And on the march to relieve Gordon at Khartoum. Royal Sussex Regiment, you know." Wheatley didn't know and he couldn't see what it had to do with the case he needed to get on with. The Colonel continued. "That's where I got this," indicating his leg.

That explains the limp, Wheatley thought, but not why he was sitting listening to an old soldier's reminiscences. He decided to try a direct approach.

"Excuse me, sir, but who exactly are you and why are you here?"

"Direct and to the point, I like that in a man, Detective Wheatley." Wheatley waited but when no more information was forthcoming, repeated his question.

"Sorry, thought I said. Colonel Gervaise St John Percy Gray, late of the Royal Sussex Regiment. And more pertinently in your case, Grand Master of the Lodge you shouldn't know anything about. Cronin tells me you need help with that charlatan Hughes-Lewthwaite."

Wheatley closed his eyes and for the first time in his short career with the Brighton Municipal Constabulary, mentally thanked the Inspector of Detectives.

"Did you know him well, sir?"

"Tolerably. Ran into him at salons, theatres, the races and so on. And of course, at the…" Colonel Gray allowed a cough to replace the last word in his sentence, then continued. "Never took to him. We sometimes get fellows attending meetings who are down for the Season, but he never struck me as quite right."

"Like me, sir? With my handshake?"

"Oh no, nothing like that. He was very convincing in that way. No. It was that he never seemed quite the gentleman. Always soliciting for drinks, that sort of thing. Disappearing when it was his shout. Never trust a chap who doesn't stand his round, or reneges on his Mess-bill."

"Did he ever ask you for money?" asked Wheatley.

"Not me, no. But a few of the fellows got their fingers burned, I believe. Though that sort of thing went on at social occasions."

"Could you give me some names of those with burned fingers?"

"Of course not."

Wheatley met Colonel Gray's eyes and realised he would get nowhere pursuing that line of enquiry.

"And his niece, sir? Did you meet her at all?"

"Oh yes. The lovely Stephanie. When he first arrived, he seemed to be hawking her around like a pimp. Excuse my language, young man. That stopped later, though."

"Would you recognise her?" asked Wheatley, reaching into his pocket for the two likenesses. He handed the photograph of the woman found on the beach and Pettit's drawing as described by Millie to the Colonel. Colonel Gray looked carefully at them and handed the drawing back to Wheatley.

"No idea who that is, but this," he said, holding up the photograph, "is the woman I knew as Miss Stephanie Hughes-Lewthwaite. Not a flattering likeness, but certainly her." He looked at the photograph again. "Taken post-mortem, was it?"

"Well, yes. How did you…"

"Don't look so surprised. I'm a soldier. Or I was. Seen plenty of dead bodies in my time. They all have the same look when the soul retreats from their eyes." The Colonel sat still, looking into space. Wheatley assumed that he was remembering lost comrades and allowed him time. After a couple of minutes of silence, Colonel Gray roused himself, stood and said, "Well, if that is all, Detective Constable."

"Just one thing, sir," said Wheatley, also rising to his feet. "You said, in your words, that Hughes-Lewthwaite was 'hawking his niece around' but that stopped. Do you know why?"

"Chap stayed after the Season. Most unusual. But even before the end things changed. At first his niece was always on his arm at social occasions and he was very happy to allow her into the company of other gentlemen while he concluded what he called 'a little piece of business.' But as time went on, we saw her less and less. He attended a lot of social occasions alone. Several of the younger chaps were awfully disappointed, I can tell you. And not just the younger ones. When she did attend, he didn't let her out of his sight. If you ask me, he became besotted by her. His own niece!"

"Besotted?" asked Wheatley.

"You know the sort of thing. Having a reasonable conversation with the chap and he isn't paying attention. His eyes watching her every move. Same at the dinner table. And if she left the room, well! Like a raw recruit before battle. Didn't relax until she returned."

Wheatley thanked the Colonel, his mind trying to insert this new aspect of Charlie Runcorn into the narrative of his investigation. As Colonel Gray made his way towards the office door, he stumbled slightly. "Damned leg!" he said. Then, "Ah, just the thing." An umbrella stand stood by the door and in it was the Malacca cane

Wheatley kept meaning to return to Jakub Zimmerman. Colonel Gray rested his weight on the cane for a moment, then used it to support his wounded leg as he left the room.

"Sir, that cane is needed…".

"Don't worry, young man. I'll see the good Inspector gets it back," said the Colonel as he exited through the door.

Friday 23rd February 1894

Wheatley was on early shifts and had spent the morning clearing up a few matters which had become outstanding since he had been fully occupied with the disappearance and murders. He knew that he was prevaricating and from time to time his eyes flicked to the correspondence he had received that morning from Detective Winstanley of the Metropolitan Police Force. Try as he might, he couldn't help thinking of the consequences of its contents. He really needed to talk to someone about the case and although Inspector Cronin had climbed in Wheatley's estimation with his facilitating of the interview with the Grand Master of the Lodge Charlie Runcorn had infiltrated in his guise of Sir Cecil Hughes-Lewthwaite, his upper-class prejudices and propensity for taking short cuts were not what Wheatley needed. It was with some relief, therefore, that he saw Detective Edwards enter the Office a full ten minutes before his shift was due to begin.

"Afternoon, Wheatley," said Edwards, divesting himself of his outside wear.

Wheatley picked up Winstanley's letter and moved to the other side of the desk as Edwards took possession of the chair and removed the Daily Log from the shelf behind him.

"Anything urgent I should know about?" he asked, opening the Log.

"I've been thinking about the murders and what you said yesterday, about who I believe," said Wheatley. "But I can't help thinking the question ought to be, 'Who has something to gain from the deceptions and murders'."

"Well, who does gain?" asked Edwards at the same time engrossed in the Daily Log.

"Until now I couldn't see anyone with a motive, except possibly an unknown victim of Charlie Runcorn's confidence tricks. But why kill the girl, whether she turns out to be Miss Stephanie or not?"

"Until now?" asked Edwards, closing the Log and looking interested for the first time.

"This morning I received this from Detective Winstanley," said Wheatley, handing a sheet of paper to Edwards. "He apologises for the delay but says Piccadilly is in an adjoining district which meant his inspector had to talk with Piccadilly's inspector before Winstanley was able to make his enquiries."

Edwards took the letter and silently read it. The information it contained was short and to the point. Susan Stephens had been an exemplary employee at Messrs. Swann and Edgar for four years and five months. She had boarded at one of the establishment's lodging houses for female employees. Then, one day in May last year, she hadn't turned up for work. Her room was just as she had left it, all her things still there. But she hadn't been seen since.

"Susan Stephens disappeared from view in London at approximately the same time Millicent Stephens appeared as a maid in the house on the Steyne rented by Charlie Runcorn," said Wheatley.

"Bit flimsy, isn't it?" said Edwards. "Could be just a coincidence of two people with the common name of Stephens."

"Yes," agreed Wheatley. "But there are a few too many coincidences for my liking. Firstly, a man called Cecil de Vere rents a house from the Regency Lettings Agency ten years or so ago. His maid, Millicent Stephens, adored older sister of the said Susan Stephens, dies as a result of an illegal abortion which he arranged. Ten years later, Sir Tobias Hughes-Lewthwaite rents a house for the Brighton Season, again from the Regency Lettings Agency. A maid, also called Millicent Stephens, turns up at the house at the exact same time as Susan Stephens goes missing from her employment and lodgings in London. And in the final coincidence, Pettit the artist agrees with me that the handwriting of Cecil de Vere and Sir Tobias Hughes-Lewthwaite obtained from the Regency Lettings Agency are identical. Suggesting that they are one and the same person, to whit a confidence trickster called Charlie Runcorn."

"Who is now adorning a cold slab in the mortuary watched over by the estimable Shadrach Mears," said Edwards. "Even so, are you suggesting that little Millie could be involved in this? Really? Even a murderess?"

"Far-fetched, I know," agreed Wheatley. "And Doctor Buchanan admitted that it was very unlikely that a woman could exert enough pressure to throttle a large man like Charlie Runcorn into unconsciousness."

"Not to mention the callousness for all that stabbing afterwards. Not very ladylike," shivered Edwards.

"However, I do think Millie has questions to answer," said Wheatley. "And I have unfinished business in Miss Stephanie's bedroom."

"Aye, aye."

"Not at all what you are thinking, Edwards. It's just that at the back of my mind something Doctor Buchanan said about the stabbings is connecting with what I saw in the bedroom that first night. If only I could put my finger on it."

Edwards was still smirking as Wheatley left the room, but recovered sufficiently to say, "Better take one of Sergeant Johnson's boys with you. If the lovely Millie *is* involved, have you thought she might have an accomplice? A big one."

Monday 26th February 1894

"I'm sorry to be dragging you this way again, Mr Jupp."

"Don't you worry about that, Mr Wheatley. Makes a change from the same old, same old."

Wheatley had taken to heart Detective Edward's warning about possible large accomplices, and this was the fourth day in a row that he and PC Jupp had made the journey from the Town Hall Police Station to number 28, Grand Parade. Today, as on all the other days, there had been no answer to their knocking and no evidence of occupation that they could see by peering through the windows. "I think she's definitely done a bunk," PC Jupp said, and Wheatley had to admit that he was probably right. Peering up at the blank windows on this cold but clear Monday, Wheatley made a decision.

"I think you can return to the Town Hall, Mr Jupp," he said. "I'll make my way over to the Regency Lettings Agency and get a set of keys. I really need to look inside."

"I think it better if I accompany you," said the Police Constable. "After all, we don't know if there isn't someone hiding inside and Sergeant Johnson would have my guts for garters if anything happened to you."

"Indeed, we wouldn't want to upset the irascible Sergeant Johnson," said Wheatley.

"Just across the Steyne there's a tobacconist who stocks my favourite shag at a very reasonable price," continued PC Jupp. "Perhaps we could call in on the way to the letting agency?"

"You pop across there now, Mr Jupp," said Wheatley. "I'll wait here just in case she's out shopping or something."

"Very well, lad. Shan't be long."

As the happy policeman set off across the Steyne, Wheatley stood gazing at the house, letting his mind stray over the case. He couldn't really believe that Millicent Stephens could be involved in murder. But she certainly seemed to have misled him here and there. Perhaps just confusion as Inspector Cronin had suggested. But then, why did it seem that she had disappeared? And what was nagging him about Dr Buchanan and Miss Stephanie's bedroom? As he stood deep in thought he heard a door open and a familiar voice say, "Is that you, detective? What are *you* doing here?"

"Millie!" Wheatley was so surprised at her suddenly appearing in the front doorway of 28, Grand Parade that all of his resolution to be formal and professional when he next met her disappeared and he positively squeaked her name. "Where have you been?" he asked. "And why didn't you answer the door before? We've been knocking for the past four days."

"Oh, was that you?" said Millie. "I peeped out and saw a dirty great copper knocking on the door, and well, I'm not that fond of rozzers, so I kept quiet."

"Millie, I'm a copper. I mean, a policeman."

"Oh, you don't count, detective. So, you coming in or what?"

As he reached the top of the steps to the entrance, Wheatley remembered Detective Edwards' warning and the absence of PC Jupp. "Are you alone?" he asked.

"Not now you're here," said Millie, standing aside so that he could enter.

Once inside, Wheatley's resolve to keep the interview professional returned. "Miss Stephens," he began.

"So formal," mused Millie, moving close to him to remove a speck of something from the shoulder of his overcoat. "Aren't you even going to take your hat off?" she asked, examining the offending fleck before flicking it from her finger to the floor and looking up and smiling at him.

"Millie," said Wheatley, removing his hat and looking around for somewhere to put it. Millie took his bowler from him and placed it on the hall stand. Taking advantage of her turned back, Wheatley continued, "I have to ask you some questions, but first I need to go upstairs."

"Is this coming off too?" asked Millie, fingering his topcoat's lapel and looking up with her teeth disconcertingly biting her lower lip. Wheatley hurriedly removed his overcoat which Millie hung up before saying, "So Mr Policeman, you wish me to accompany you upstairs? Such a tempting offer. A pity I have so much work to do. Unfortunately, I'm very busy this morning."

"No need to interrupt your work, I'll manage perfectly well on my own," said Wheatley, moving around Millie and positively bolting up the stairs.

Wheatley paused outside of Miss Stephanie's room and thought about the last time he had stood here as Millie had turned into Sir Toby's room on St Valentine's Eve. He knew he had followed, telling her she was going into the wrong room. After that he remembered nothing. Nothing at all, until he had woken in Sir Toby's bed the next morning. Forcing down the guilt about what he had possibly done in those blank times, Wheatley took a deep breath and opened the door to Miss Stephanie's bedroom. The room looked much as it had the first time he had seen it and he swivelled around slowly trying to remember what had piqued his interest. His eyes passed over the dressing table, on to the washstand, and then returned to the dressing table. Something was stirring in his mind. Standing in front of the dressing table he checked his memory. Same pots, bottles and trays containing make-up, perfume and cheap jewellery. Same necklaces hanging on the mirror stanchions. And as he gazed into the looking glass a picture came to him. Of Dr Buchanan standing in front of a mirror in the snug of the Sudeley Arms saying "*Cherchez la Femme,*" and fixing her hat onto her head with hat pins. Of her report of the stabbing with an unknown long, slender, circular object. Of particularly sturdy hat pins decorated with peacock feathers he had seen in the centre drawer of Miss Stephanie's dressing table!

As Wheatley pulled open the drawer, he heard the bedroom door open and he turned to see that Millie had followed him after all.

"And there was me thinking it was me you were interested in," she said.

"Oh, it is," said Wheatley. "After I've found what I am looking for, we need to have a long talk."

"What about?" asked Millie.

'Well, firstly about why you told me that Mr and Mrs Garson lived in faraway Kent when in fact they live along the coast just a short train ride from Brighton."

"Do they?" said Millie. "I didn't take much notice to be honest. He was always sounding off about something and she would wait, then put him in his place. Sure they said something about Kent, though."

Wheatley wasn't in the mood for excuses. So many of the inconsistencies of this case were boiling up inside of him. "Also about a body that you say isn't Miss Stephanie but others say is," he continued. "About Millicent Stephens of Hassocks who worked for the Regency Letting Agency ten years ago. And while we're on the subject of the Regency Letting Agency, about why they deny all knowledge of you and think that this property is empty and locked up for the winter."

"Them's a lot of questions," said Millie.

"That's not the half of it," said Wheatley, turning back to look into the dressing table drawer. "I haven't even mentioned Sir Tobias Hughes-Lewthwaite who you worked for or Cecil de Vere who the other Millie worked for, and who happens to be one and the same person."

"I'm sorry to hear that, detective."

Wheatley was scrabbling about in the back of the drawer refusing to admit that the hatpins he now remembered so clearly were not there while a verbal tirade of the conflicting evidence poured from him. He felt Millie move close behind him. Telling himself to keep focussed, he determined to continue demonstrating why he needed explanations from her.

"Nor have I approached the murder of Sir Tobias and the mysterious appearance of his 'wife'. Or asked about Susan Stephens of Hassocks, sister of the other Millicent Stephens, who disappeared from her London lodgings and employment at the same time you arrived here!"

"Oh, I am so sorry to hear that, detective," repeated Millie. He felt her press her body into his back and drop her hands gently onto his shoulders.

"And don't think your feminine wiles will distract me this time," said Wheatley, more to convince himself than Millie. But as he moved to turn back towards her, he realised that it was not just Millie's hands that had landed on his shoulders and that something was tightening around his throat. Almost in disbelief he raised his hands to his neck and found a double cord already too tight to get his fingers underneath, though he scrabbled uselessly at it until his neck tissues swelled over it and he could feel blood seeping under his fingernails. *Think!* he screamed at himself and feeling he should be able to overpower a slight young woman, reached back over his shoulders meaning to grab the hands that were pulling on the cords. His hands found nothing. No matter how he stretched, he couldn't reach her, couldn't even touch her. Wheatley knew that Millie was close behind him and that the ligature around his throat was cutting off his air supply and that he ought to be able to reach her and wrest the cords from her, but it was getting more and more difficult to think and he couldn't suck air any further than his tongue and try as he might he couldn't reach far enough back to overpower her. But he was bigger and heavier than her and so desperately he threw himself backwards hoping to crush her beneath him and so force her to relinquish her hold. Millie did fall beneath him but the agony around his throat and the burning in his lungs were not mitigated. As he fell, his legs kicked upwards, demolishing the flimsy dressing table and its mirror with its seven years of bad luck, smashing the pots, trays and bottles as they crashed to the floor so that instead of oxygen his nose was suffused by the musk and sickly sweetness of scent as he continued to claw backwards until his arms would work no more and a blackness claimed him.

*

He was being shaken. And none too gently. Forcing his eyes open, he was aware of a human shape and a frantic voice saying, "Wheatley, Wheatley, speak to me, lad." As he sat up, he took a deep whooshing breath in through his mouth and heard a distant "Thank the Lord." His eyes were streaming and the pain in them was only matched by his pulsing head and rasping throat. When he raised a hand to clear his eyes in order to see better, it was blood, not tears that he wiped away. The shaker had risen to his feet and was now hauling Wheatley up too. Wheatley had a moment to notice that his awakener was PC Jupp when his world turned upside down. Literally. It took a while to realise that he was dangling over the police constable's shoulder as Jupp descended the stairs and out through a battered-looking front door. Wheatley tried to protest, to form words, to insist that they needed to search the house. That there was a murderess at large. But all that came out of his mouth was a harsh gurgle that felt as if it was ripping his throat apart. By this time PC Jupp was in the road hailing a cab and dumping Wheatley none to gently onto the seat. As the cabbie cracked his whip and the horse lurched into a trot, Wheatley again tried to make Jupp see sense but even if he had been able to form words instead of an incomprehensible grunting, he doubted that he would have got through to the constable who was fully occupied holding Wheatley down onto the seat whilst simultaneously screaming at the cabbie to drive faster.

Less than five minutes later the steaming horse shuddered to a halt outside of the Sussex County Hospital and Wheatley found himself roughly jerked from the cab and once again over PC Jupp's shoulder as the constable stumbled through the hospital entrance yelling for help. Within seconds Wheatley had been placed onto a trolley, still trying to explain an urgent need to return to the house to apprehend a criminal whilst actually grunting like a madman. His efforts caused a large orderly to lay across him to keep him still while the noise and chaos around him seemed to increase as suddenly he felt a sharp pain in his left arm. Gradually a feeling of warmth flushed through him, and for the second time that day, blackness descended.

Tuesday 27th February 1894

Wheatley became aware of several things at once. That his head was throbbing. That he had a raging thirst, but when he tried swallowing the limited amount of saliva in his mouth, his throat screamed in pain. That he was lying in a bed whose covers tightly bound him to the mattress and someone was holding his hand. No, not his hand, his wrist. But worst of all… Worse than the pain and disorientation was that he couldn't open his eyes. Frightened by his apparent blindness, he struggled to sit upright, only to find a hand pressing firmly on his chest holding him in place, a man's voice saying, "Easy matey," and a softer, female one saying, "Lie still while we sort you out."

He had little choice held by the heavy hand on his chest and the restrictive bed covers and so he lay listening to a metallic chink and the sound of pouring liquid. Then he felt something soft and wet being passed gently across his eyes, and as the sluicing continued, he felt his eyelids lift and light flood his vision, revealing blurred images that slowly settled into focus. A large man crouched over him, holding him down, a woman looking on.

"I think you can let him go now, Detective Edwards," said Dr Buchanan, placing an enamelled kidney dish containing a bloodstained cloth on the table Wheatley could see next to the bed.

"I thought I was blind," croaked Wheatley at the expense of a searing pain in his throat. He moved his hand to his neck but only had time to feel that it was heavily bandaged before Dr Buchanan took hold of his wrist, removing it from the bandaging.

"Certainly a better response than 'where am I?'," she said, holding Wheatley's wrist in one hand and a watch in the other. "Just your eyelids gummed up from the bleeding; nasty gash on your eye-brow. You must have hit your head as you fell," she said matter-of-factly, before adding, "Your pulse is stronger than it ought to be, and before you get round to asking where you are, you are in the hospital and seemingly recovering well."

"Millie?" Wheatley said, trying to rise. His throat was so sore and his head throbbed as he sank back, exhausted.

"Don't you worry about that, it'll be sorted," said Edwards.

"Rest now," said the doctor and despite wanting answers to so many questions, Wheatley could not prevent himself sinking back into unconsciousness.

When he awoke several hours later, Wheatley found that things were far from sorted. There had been no sign of Millie in the house.

"PC Jupp saw you weren't where he'd left you and decided to wait. When he heard crashing from inside the house, he broke the door down and was up the stairs so quickly she couldn't have passed him," said Detective

Edwards. "There was no sign of her in either bedroom. He tried both before he found you."

Wheatley was examining impressions in his head. The feeling of helplessness and fear as he slipped unconscious. The image of PC Jupp looming over him saying "Thank the Lord" as Wheatley found himself able to breathe again. The scramble to the hospital. And then the blankness until he had woken that morning.

"How?" was all he managed before the pain in his throat grew too much.

"She used a turn-key," said Edwards.

"Tourniquet," corrected Dr Buchanan.

"She used this," said Edwards, holding up one of the stout hat pins topped by the eye of a peacock feather that Wheatley had been searching for in Miss Stephanie's bedroom when the attack happened. "She used it to wind in a bit of string to tighten it more than even a man could do with his bare hands."

"A lace, not string. String could have broken," said Dr Buchanan. "Actually, a corset lace. They need to be strong to cinch in waists to the extent they do. The police constable who found you was able to release the tourniquet so you could breathe but the lace was so embedded in your throat tissue that we had to remove that here. Caused a bit of a mess, hence the bandaging."

Wheatley moved his hand towards his neck but once again Dr Buchanan stopped him. "Don't touch," she said. "There is a lot of swelling at the moment but that will go down in a week or so. The bruising to your larynx and scarring from the lace will take a little longer."

"How long here?" managed Wheatley.

"Oh, you should be able to be discharged in the next couple of days. Sooner if possible. I called in a lot of favours to get this room for you, and Dr Littlejohn, my colleague whose bed it is, has patients lined up for it."

"Inspector Cronin has arranged for Detective Wheatley to be transferred to the new Police Convalescent Home in Hove as soon as you think he's up to it," said Edwards.

"Excellent!" Dr Buchanan held out her hand and took the hat pin from Detective Edwards. "At least she didn't stab you like she did the others," she said to Wheatley. "Either she didn't want you dead or she was disturbed before she could use this. I've tried it in the wounds — it *is* the murder weapon. Or something very similar."

Wheatley watched as the doctor returned the hat-pin to Detective Edwards, realising that the new science of finger-printing would be useless with so many people having handled the murder weapon while at the same time trying to convince himself that Millie had let him live deliberately. Surely Millie would not want him dead? So many thoughts mingled with a feeling of betrayal that he again felt exhaustion creeping over him. He needed to rest.

Friday 2nd March 1894

Wheatley had spent two days in the recently built Police Convalescent Home in Portland Road, Hove, unable to sleep. The dormitory he was assigned to was mainly for police officers suffering from tuberculosis, sent there by police forces from London and the South East of England in the hope that sea air might alleviate their symptoms. While the men were pleasant enough, their constant coughing and spluttering so disturbed the detective that he discharged himself and walked the few hundred yards to his lodgings in Clarendon Villas. Here he was fussed over by the attentive Mrs Lee and given considerable licence by the formidable Mrs Harris, even being allowed to have supper served in bed on his first evening. Now he was ambulatory and determined to be back to work that weekend. And for a very good reason.

*

Wheatley had often wondered why the shelters erected on the seafront for the convenience of visitors had seats all around them. Only those at the front and sides afforded a vista of the sea. Why would anyone want to sit with their back to the view? Today he had found the answer. It was a pleasant-looking bright day, but a cold wind was gusting mightily from the south. Sitting on the 'wrong' side meant he was sheltered from the icy blast and without the maelstrom, the weather felt quite balmy. He had even considered removing his hat. Wheatley sat watching Pettit ply his trade on Hove Lawns. Currently he was kneeling beside an ancient dowager feverishly sketching while her dog circled and periodically jumped up at him, yapping constantly. Presumably the woman assumed that Pettit had an affinity with dogs to cause such affection. Wheatley knew that Pettit always filled his pockets with meat scraps when out on assignment and it was the odour of these that made her darling so friendly towards him. The artist was often at the boarding house during the day and Wheatley had appreciated Pettit's kindness during his convalescence. He was just musing on how good it felt to have a friend when Pettit stood and walked towards the shelter. The dog tried to follow but was prevented from doing so by the lead held firmly by its owner who proceeded to drag it away in the opposite direction, still yapping furiously. Pettit ripped a page from his sketch book, crumpled it in his hand and threw it to the floor before casting himself down on the seat next to Wheatley.

"No luck?" asked Wheatley, bending to retrieve the cast-off drawing. "It's really very good," he said, smoothing the paper out on his lap.

"Good or not, I could see there was no way she was going to pay for it. Slim pickings today," said Pettit. "Your voice sounds better today, though. Not so rough."

Wheatley placed a finger gently under his chin and drew it down his neck, tracing the slowly healing wounds. "It's getting better every day, but these marks are likely to be with me a while longer."

"And you're still determined to return to work this weekend?" asked Pettit.

"Yes," said Wheatley.

"Something to do with the case?"

"Yes," said Wheatley.

"And you're not going to tell me what?"

"No," said Wheatley.

The two men sat in silence following that until Pettit said, "So my portrait was no use after all? She was making it up, just stringing me along?"

"Yes," said Wheatley.

"Pity, so much for my career as police artist."

"She was a lovely girl, though," said Pettit a little later still. "If it hadn't been so obvious she was keen on you, I'd have made a try for her myself."

"Keen on me? She tried to kill me!" said Wheatley. "I believe it was all an act to deflect suspicion from herself."

"I'm not so sure," said Pettit. "Unless she's a greater actress than Sarah Bernhardt, she was certainly keen on you, whatever happened later. I could tell."

Wheatley wondered if that was true, but rapidly dismissed the thought. It was unimportant in terms of the case and that was what mattered now.

"Come on, old chap, time to make our weary way home," said Pettit rising. Wheatley stood and the two companions set off across the Lawns together.

"I do hope it's not faggots again for supper," said Pettit.

Sunday 4th March 1894

Wheatley consulted his watch as he walked from Hassocks railway station. It was just after eleven in the morning. Six minutes past eleven to be precise, he noted. The detective knew the village had no church of its own and was split between the parishes of Clayton and Keymer. This meant that Hassocks was almost deserted on this Sunday when, by tradition, English men and women who were able returned to their church of baptism, their mother church, for a service of celebration. Many no longer living at home also took the chance to visit their actual mothers at the same time. So much so that there were grumbles from within the church that the original meaning of the fourth Sunday of Lent was being lost and the Mothering Sunday service was now merely a forbear of a much-anticipated Sunday lunch with the family. When his father had been dominant in the religious squabbles which wracked his childhood, Wheatley had attended the church of his baptism on this day. Nowadays though, he paid lip-service to the expectations of both his landladies and his profession and would normally have been seated in the congregation of St. Andrews, Hove on any Sunday he was not working. *How*, he wondered, *does a boy brought up as a Judaeo-Catholic find it necessary to conform to the expectations of society by attending a Church of England place of worship as a man?* Wheatley had been thinking about his life a lot recently. It made him uncomfortable. And as always when the discomfort of feelings assaulted him, he turned his mind to other things. Specifically to work. Work which today, he felt, was not going to be its usual comforting self. Today work was likely to bring distress of its own.

Lost in thought, Wheatley found himself outside of the Village Smithy, a sign stating 'George Small, Blacksmith and Farrier' suspended over the open shop-front. As expected, the forge was cold and the blacksmith absent. To make sure, Wheatley made his way past the forge and the attached dwelling house to the stable behind. Seeing that George's trap was missing and the pony stall unoccupied, he made his way back to the front of the shop to wait in the early spring sunshine. Wheatley needed transport but he had not contacted the blacksmith beforehand for fear that he might alert the Widow Stephens. No, he would just have to wait until George returned before pressing him and his pony and trap into the service of the Brighton Municipal Constabulary.

Pressing the blacksmith into service proved easier to say than to do. Wheatley had had to wait over an hour before the pony and trap eventually rattled into sight. Even then, George had tried to by-pass the detective, forcing Wheatley to step in front of the conveyance. It took two shiny half-crowns and a lot of persuasion with the blacksmith complaining that he had already been to

Keymer and back that morning and that he was 'ready fer m'dinner' before Wheatley was seated in the trap and on his way to Meadow Farm. Needless to say, there was no conversation and a distinct lack of bonhomie during the journey.

The arrival at Meadow Farm was similar to Wheatley's previous visit. George drove the trap into the dilapidated barn, then jumped down to take a nose-bag to his pony. Wheatley trekked through the chickens pecking desultorily at the ground, thankful that this time he had avoided a deluge. The sun was shining, and the farmyard mud baked to the hardness of concrete. He paused in the farmhouse porch, remembering that last time the door had been locked and Mrs Stephens had said that visitors 'usually come round the back.' However, as he was on official business, he decided that to use the front door was appropriate. He knocked loudly and was eventually rewarded by a call of 'just a minute,' from inside.

It seemed in fact several minutes before the door was opened by Mrs Stephens. She was wearing an elegant dark skirt with a frivolous primrose-coloured blouse and a nervous look. Once again Wheatley noted how unlike his stereotypical image of a farmer's wife she seemed, though this time she *was* wearing an apron, frantically rubbing it between her hands.

"Detective Wheatley. What are you doing here today of all days?"

"Good afternoon, Mrs Stephens. If I could possibly come in for a minute or so?"

"Well, I'm a bit busy at the moment," said the widow, glancing over her shoulder, "if you could come back tomorrow?"

"If you don't mind," said Wheatley, moving forwards so that the poor woman had to give way, "it will only take a moment."

The detective made his way into the farmhouse kitchen, Mrs Stephens bustling in after him. After looking around frantically at what were obviously the remains of a Sunday lunch, she appeared to relax a little. Taking a deep breath she said, "Now, what can I do for you Mr Wheatley?"

"Actually, Mrs Stephens, it isn't you I wanted to see."

"No? Well, what are you doing here then?"

"I was hoping to have a word with Mi… Susan."

"With who?"

"With Susan, your daughter."

Mrs Stephens paused at this point, her upper teeth exposed, biting her lower lip. Not, Wheatley noted, in the coquettish way her younger daughter he knew as Millie had the last time he had met her, but in a sign of anxiety.

"I don't know why you thought you'd find her here. I live alone. Anyone can tell you that. I haven't seen Susan in ages. So, if that's all you've come for…"

Mrs Stephens had moved to the kitchen door and was holding it open, obviously expecting the detective to leave. Wheatley theatrically swivelled on his heel, hoping to turn a full circle while giving the impression that he was examining every corner of the room. He almost made it but had to grab at the back of a chair to steady himself as he stumbled over the final few degrees.

"Detective," said Mrs Stephens still holding the kitchen door with one hand while indicating the passage to the front door with the other. Wheatley regained his balance and remained where he was.

Mrs Stephens was the first to speak. "I told you last time. Susan works in London. I think I have the address somewhere." She left the door ajar and moved towards the dresser drawer where Wheatley remembered she had previously stored the postcard from Susan Stephens he had been shown on his last visit.

"She hasn't been seen in London since last May," he said to the widow's back. She didn't turn around but her scrabbling in the dresser drawer stilled. Wheatley moved to stand beside the kitchen table. "Table containing the remains of a meal for two. Roast lamb, if I'm not mistaken. You eat well, Mrs Stephens." Mrs Stephens had not moved. "Two cup and saucers set out for tea, fresh flowers on the windowsill," Wheatley continued. "And you told me yourself, Susan never misses visiting on your birthday in May, at Christmas or on Mothering Sunday."

"Which is today," he added after a pause to see if he would get a reaction. Mrs Stephens turned to face the detective. She was rolling her apron in her hands and once or twice she opened her mouth as if to say something, but no words came out. Wheatley stood and waited.

"Very clever, detective," said a voice. "I wondered if I might be seeing you today."

Both Wheatley and Mrs Stephens whirled round, overlapping words bursting from them.

"Susan!" said Mrs Stephens.

"Millie!" said Wheatley.

Susan/Millie stood in the doorway. Her hair was held up by ivory combs and she wore a smart skirt and white blouse which showed a glimpse of decolletage through the lace that trimmed it. Wheatley knew he should be taking some sort of action, but he gaped, rooted to the spot as Millie/Susan passed him by to take the hands of her now crying mother and he caught the sweet earthiness of her perfume.

"Susan, no, I told you to hide," sobbed Mrs Stephens. "I tried to get rid of him, I really did."

"It's all right, Ma," said Susan. "I was expecting this. To be honest, it had to happen sometime and I'm glad it's sooner rather than later. And now it's happened, I realise it's what I want. Honest, Ma." Susan had moved her hands to her mother's shoulders and bent forward to kiss her wet cheeks. Then she turned and strode purposefully towards the detective.

"Millie... Susan..." was all Wheatley could utter.

"And you can stay right there, Mr Small," she said as she breezed past, shedding that disturbing perfume in her wake. Wheatley turned to follow her progress to see that the blacksmith had entered unobserved through the back door and was quietly moving towards him, a large club-hammer in his hand. Wonderment that such a big man could move so quietly mixed in Wheatley's head with an inner voice screaming at him to run, to hide. To fight if necessary. But to do anything except stand rooted to the spot, his mouth agape. Fortunately, Susan took charge. Placing herself between the blacksmith and the detective she said, reaching out for the hammer, "It's all right, Mr Small, it's what I want. I just want to get it all over with."

It was probably only a few seconds, but to Wheatley it seemed like many long minutes that he held his breath until the blacksmith gave a sharp nod and relinquished his hold. Susan placed the hammer on the table amidst the lunch detritus and turned back to the blacksmith.

"Thank you, George," she said. "If I'm old enough to call you George now after all these years of Mr Small."

"Susan," was all the blacksmith said. He had not taken his eyes off of Wheatley during the whole incident and he continued to stare at the detective as Susan, assuming permission, said, "Now, George, you stay here and have a cup of tea with Ma. Me and the Detective Constable here are going outside for a talk. When we come back, we will need you to drive us to the station to catch the Brighton train."

For a moment Wheatley wondered whether the blacksmith still intended to do him violence despite Susan's calming words, but she took George's arm and pulled out a chair for him and eventually he sat down, placing his meaty forearms on the kitchen table with a sigh.

"That's right," she said, briefly placing a hand on his shoulder. Then, turning to her mother said, "Put the kettle

231

on for you and Mr Small, Ma. Mr Wheatley and me won't want none. We'll be just outside."

Next, it was Wheatley's arm that Susan took, leading him out of the farmhouse through the back door. They emerged into Mrs Stephens' vegetable garden. The plot was bordered by neatly dug beds, the first green shoots showing through the dark earth. The beds were backed by fruit bushes and at the centre of the garden stood a wizened apple tree surrounded by a small patch of grass. There was a hint of green in the buds swelling on the tree's branches and beneath stood a roughly made bench. It was to this that Susan led the detective.

They sat, side by side, neither speaking, both staring ahead. The sun was warm for early spring and from somewhere in the bushes a blackbird sang. Wheatley felt Susan gently touch his neck where the livid marks of the lace and the bruising were still healing.

"That looks sore," she said.

"Yes," said Wheatley.

The silence lasted a little longer before Susan said, "I never wanted to hurt you, detective, but you're too clever for your own good. When I realised you knew the truth, I panicked, thought I had to get away somehow."

Wheatley reflected that he certainly hadn't 'known the truth', at least not until the noose had settled around his neck. But he *had* had suspicions. Suspicions that he'd perhaps repressed because of personal feelings.

"So really it was your fault," Susan continued breaking into the detective's thoughts. Wheatley turned to look at her.

"And the other victims, was it their fault too?"

"He was a right bastard that Cecil de Vere or whatever he called himself. He as good as killed Millie and Faith." Susan's voice betrayed a tenseness, a repressed anger.

"Faith?" asked Wheatley.

"Millie's daughter. We named her after my mother. We couldn't put the poor thing into her grave without a name. It was bad enough she couldn't be christened."

Wheatley nodded. "Runcorn, that was de Vere's real name, Charlie Runcorn. Granted he was wicked," he said, "but it wasn't your place to impose justice."

"An eye for an eye, detective," said Susan. "And if I hadn't done it who would? Your lot? You've had ten years to do that and done nothing." There were tears shining in Susan's eyes now, either of anger or reminiscence. Wheatley couldn't tell which. He bit back the retort that it wasn't him who had ignored the crime.

"And the young woman? Did she deserve to die? She was with child, too, you know."

Susan sat back at that. Her face contorted and the tears in her eyes began to fall. She appeared to be having difficulty swallowing and her responses were indistinct, but Wheatley caught "...tried to warn her..." and "...shouldn't have laughed at ..." between the sobs before her voice petered out and she sat breathing heavily and staring at the ground. Wheatley removed his pocket handkerchief and held it out to her. She sat holding it until her breathing settled and her tears subsided. Then she used the handkerchief to wipe carefully under her eyes, blot her cheeks, and finally, blow her nose. And not too daintily either.

"Thank you, I don't suppose you'll want this back," she said, holding out the wet handkerchief.

"I will, thank you," said Wheatley, and taking it he tucked the handkerchief into a shirt pocket beneath his waistcoat. "I have a small bag of clothing laundered every fortnight as part of my tenancy agreement," he said. "It will come out as new." As soon as he began to speak, he was cringing inside, wondering why he was maundering on about laundry and not getting on with the job in hand. His embarrassment became more acute as Susan said with a wet, unconvincing levity, "And there I was, thinking you was keeping it to remind you of me, you placing it next to your heart and all."

Wheatley felt his colour rising and became officious to offset it. "Miss Stephens," he said, "I must caution you that you are to be questioned about the murders of Charles Runcorn, known to you as Sir Tobias Hughes-Lewthwaite, baronet, and the person known as the honourable Miss Stephanie Hughes-Lewthwaite..." and meant to continue. But he was cut off by Susan.

"Don't you come the high horse with me, detective. Not after... well, you know!"

"Millie... I mean, Susan..."

"Back to first names, that's an improvement. I think we'd better stick with Susan for now. To avoid confusion, you see? Now ask your questions. But be polite. Ask me nicely and I'll tell you no lies."

"Firstly, Susan," said Wheatley mildly, admitting defeat. "Charlie Runcorn: how did you know he would be in Brighton again this year?"

"I didn't," said Susan. "It was all one big coincidence…"

After a long story of how difficult it had been to get the Wednesday in May off from her employers for her mother's birthday and who she had to swop with and what it had cost her, Susan at last got to the point.

"So, there I was at Victoria Station waiting to get the train to Hassocks for Ma's birthday when he passes me with some tart on his arm and a porter puffing behind with a trolley piled with luggage."

"You recognised him after all those years? After all, you were very young and only saw him briefly."

"I remember as if it was yesterday. His face is printed on my memory. True, he'd aged a bit, but it was him. I was absolutely certain."

Susan went on to tell how she had followed the pair to Brighton, and then to the house on Grand Parade before returning to the station and completing her journey to Hassocks.

"I was late for Ma's birthday tea, but she forgave me. She always does."

"But why everything else?" asked Wheatley. "Why didn't you just report him? Why pretend to be a maid at the house? And how did you get away with it?"

"Report him? To who? For what? Do you think that sergeant of yours would care what happened to a servant girl ten years ago? But I knew I had to do something. Ma has kept everything of Millie's and so when I turned up at the house in Brighton dressed in one of her old uniforms — well, servants are just taken for granted. Even among other servants. It's as if they don't exist as people, just as the roles they perform. A bit like you, detective."

Wheatley did not consider that he had anything in common with a servant, but he let that remark go. "But why? What did you hope to achieve?"

"I don't know! I didn't plan it, it just happened. I suppose I wanted to see for myself what he was like up close. Perhaps I had some idea of finding evidence. Finding something about him I could use."

"And did you?"

"Well, it was obvious something crooked was going on, but I couldn't put my finger on it. I could tell she was involved at first…"

"She?" asked Wheatley.

"*Her!* Stephanie whatever she called herself. Dressing herself up to leave nothing to the imagination while simpering like a ten-year-old. Bait, I supposed. But then, towards the end of the season, it all changed. He started going out alone, and the money started to dry up. The grocer refused our orders. Eventually the gas and water were turned off."

The story Susan told mimicked that of Colonel Gray. At first Stephanie was always on Runcorn's arm, going out most evenings, often returning long after he had retired. Then a change began. He seemed more attentive, concerned for her. And she seemed to like it.

"I thought he was just keeping her sweet at first, but it was the key that convinced me."

"The key to the door between their two bedrooms? The one I found on her dressing table? You told me that they argued about it, that she used it to lock him out."

"Well, detective, I might not have told the whole truth about that. At first he had the key, and made a lot of use of it too, 'visiting' her at all hours. But then it subtly changed. He gave her the key, so she could make her own decisions. Then it was her visiting him. Often. And certainly not keeping him out."

Wheatley waited for Susan to continue. She seemed locked in thought.

"Love's young dream?" he asked eventually.

"More May with September," she said, "but they became very caught up in each other towards the end of the Season. Then he decided they were to stay on."

Susan recounted her discomfort when the staff were informed of this. "The Garsons were delighted, extra pay and free accommodation."

"But you weren't?" asked Wheatley.

"I was confused. I still didn't really know what I was doing there. I knew I had to do something, at least say something. But I let it drag on with them playing happy families and me wanting to do something but unsure what. I came home here for Christmas and almost stayed. I did stay until after New Year but went back determined not to be a coward and to say something. To confront him. I expected to be told off for being away so long and then I could have my big scene. But it was as if they hadn't noticed, and my resolve faltered. So, I just stayed on. By then I was more of a general dogsbody than a lady's maid. She hardly had any need of me any more, but just before she did her disappearing act, she called me up to her room. He was out and she needed help to lace her stays. That was when I noticed."

Susan went on to say how Stephanie had been so pleased by her pregnancy, placing her hands on her belly and smiling. "Like the cat who got the cream," she said, "though she still wanted her corset laced extra tight so she wouldn't 'show'."

"Did you say anything to her?" asked Wheatley.

"Not then, no. She was so happy, I didn't have the heart."

Wheatley wondered at this. After all, Susan *had* admitted to killing the poor young woman in a particularly savage way, but he decided to hold that line of enquiry until later.

"So you said nothing?"

"I just commented on the luggage."

238

"Luggage?"

"There was a portmanteau on the bed half full of clothes while more were folded on the bed waiting to be packed."

"But you told me nothing was missing — that the few clothes Miss Stephanie had were still in the wardrobe. When we went up to the bedroom that first evening. I remember distinctly." Wheatley's hand had crept towards his jacket pocket where he kept his notebook, but he paused as soon as he realised what he was doing, not wishing to look ridiculous consulting his notes as if in a courtroom. Susan put her hand on his arm and shook her head, smiling sadly.

"Oh, detective, what can I say?"

"So you misled me from the start."

This was a statement, not a question, but Susan still put her teeth over her bottom lip in the way that Wheatley found so disturbing and silently nodded her head in confirmation. After that it was revelation after revelation.

"That poor cow Stephanie couldn't keep a secret and at first I was pleased for her, helped her pack, find a boarding house, things like that. I was so pleased she was getting away, wouldn't end up like Millie. You see, I thought she was leaving him."

"But she wasn't?" said Wheatley.

"No, but I only found that out after she left."

Susan had overheard a conversation between Micah Garson and Sir Tobias and realised that the young and not-so-young lovers had planned to 'do a flit' and disappear together, leaving all of their debts.

"Micah Garson put the screws on him and Sir Tobias must have paid up because that Micah would sell his own mother for a shilling."

Wheatley mentally ticked off another 'witness' who had misled him, explaining why the footman had been so unhelpful from the beginning.

"But why the report to the police about a missing woman?" asked Wheatley.

"No idea," said Susan. "You're the detective."

She went on to say that once she had realised that Stephanie actually thought Sir Tobias would marry her, Susan decided to warn her about the sort of man he was.

"I sent a note to her boarding house asking to meet under the pier. I think she thought it was from him because she was all dolled up and early. When I arrived, she told me she was waiting for someone and seemed most put out when I told her I'd sent the note."

"So how did it come about? The errr…" Wheatley didn't want to use the term murder in case it stopped Susan's flow and 'killing' seemed even worse.

"The murder?" she said. "Because that's what you think it was, don't you, detective?"

"Wasn't it?"

"It was an accident," said Susan, rising from the bench and turning her back on him as she said it.

Wheatley waited and soon Susan continued, her face still hidden from view. She had told Stephanie the story of her sister and emphasised that if Sir Tobias had done it once, he would do it again. "I tried everything," she said.

"But Stephanie didn't listen?"

"Didn't listen? She ridiculed me. Showed some flashy glass ring that she said was an emerald and insisted they were engaged. Said they was going to live together. That she wouldn't end up some tart dead from a backstreet butcher like my stupid sister. That it served Millie right, silly bitch, and that I was jealous he hadn't made a go for me. I just snapped." Susan began pacing the small garden, breathing heavily, her fists clenched and her face reddening. "There was her laughing, calling me and Millie all sorts of names, and then she said, 'You can go,' like she was a real lady and I was a piece of shit to wipe off of her shoes. When she turned her back on me, I was so angry. She was wearing her velvet cloak which was too overdressed for the time of day, and she was too lazy to tie it properly. Just threw the cords over her shoulders so that they hung loosely down her back. Something made me grab them and pull." To Wheatley, Susan appeared to be reliving the occasion. Her clenched fists withdrew in unison. One knee was raised as if placed in the small of the victim's back.

"She fell back on me, but I just pulled harder and harder."

For a moment she stood there, arms bent, fists clenched as if gripping the imaginary cords. Then Susan's tension and anger seemed to fall from her, her hands flopping to her sides before she returned to the bench and sat next to the detective again, her face vacant, her hands clasped in her lap.

"And then?" said Wheatley.

"And then, I don't know."

Wheatley stared at her.

"I don't remember!" she shouted in response to the detective's quizzical look. "The next thing I know, I'm kneeling beside her on the beach, one of her fancy peacock feather hatpins in my hand, the hatpin stained with blood. There were tiny holes in her dress around the belly and she was laying there, her face turned to the sky, her eyes open, that silly velvet cloak wrapped around her neck. She wasn't breathing."

"Did no one see you? Hear the argument? Witness the struggle?"

"No one. It was a miracle, really. Too late for the day-trippers, too early for the tarts, I expect, and nearly dark by then. Even darker under the pier. I suppose I was lucky."

"If it was really an accident," said Wheatley, though he was having difficulty reconciling the word 'accident' with throttling and repeated stabbing, "why didn't you report it? Why try to cover it up?"

"I've experience of what happens when you involve coppers, remember?" said Susan. "So I thought I'd ride my luck and try to make it look like an accident."

She went on to tell how she had unwrapped the cord from around Stephanie's neck, removed the cloak and torn the fur trimming from it. This she used to disguise the strangulation marks around the victim's throat.

"The holes in her dress weren't too big and there were no bloodstains. I thought if no one bothered to remove the fur around her neck she'd be taken for some poor cow who drowned herself. Unluckily for me, you didn't believe that, did you, detective?"

Wheatley mused that he had nothing to do with the discovery of the body, or the conclusion it was more than the usual drowning. These were down to Detective Edwards and Dr Buchanan. But Millie — no, *Susan* — had seemed to see his bumbling as insight and intelligence throughout. If she hadn't, he might never have found the murderer. He stayed silent.

"I took the hatpins, what was left of the cloak and her hat and left her there under the pier. The hat and cloak I sold to some old Jew in Church Street. He gave me too much for them. Went on about how I reminded him of his favourite niece. The hatpins I kept."

For a moment they shared a silence, sitting on the bench, looking anywhere but at each other. Then Susan stood and faced the detective, her hands held out in front of her.

"I regret the death of the girl. And the…"

"Baby," Wheatley supplied.

"Yes, the…" Susan took a breath. "But him, he deserved everything he got. And more. No regrets there. So that's that, detective. Do your duty."

Wheatley wasn't at all sure that 'that' really was that. There was another murder to ask about after all. But he decided those details could wait. Susan was still standing in front of him, hands out in front of her as if anticipating something. His gaze shifted looked confusedly from her face to her hands, to her face.

"Handcuffs, detective. You do use handcuffs, don't you?"

Wheatley did. He had handcuffs. And he placed his hand over his coat pocket where they should be. But today of all days, on top of his many failings in this case and the blind luck that had got him through it, his handcuffs were securely locked in the central drawer of the desk of the Detective Office in the Brighton Police Station.

He swallowed. "I don't think we need bother with those, do we?"

"Thank you, detective," said Susan, bending to glance a kiss off his cheek. "I wouldn't want Ma's last sight of me to be in handcuffs."

Wheatley was about to say that he was sure it wouldn't be the last time her mother would see her, there being prison visits and public viewing of the trial, but he had no chance.

"Come on then or we'll miss the train," said Susan, pulling him from the bench. And so they went back to the kitchen, to the sobbing Mrs Stephens and the morose but still intimidating George Small, arm in arm and looking, Wheatley thought, more like a courting couple than a policeman and prisoner.

There was little conversation in the railway compartment which they had to themselves. Susan sat staring out of the window for most of the journey and the detective was lost in thought. At Brighton Station Wheatley did not send for a police wagon as he should have done but paid for a hansom to take them to the Town Hall. Wheatley took Susan to the cells himself.

"Not exactly comfortable, I'm sorry," he said, taking stock of the tiled walls running with damp, the board bed with its one blanket, the cracked chamber pot beneath, the heavy iron-barred door and the smell of unwashed bodies overlaid with stale alcohol and vomit.

"The last couple of years I've lived in a dormitory with fifty other shop girls stacked three to a bed and in servants' quarters in a draughty, rat-infested attic. This will do well enough," said Susan. She sat on the bed. Wheatley sat next to her.

"I suppose you want to know the rest," she said.

"Yes," said Wheatley.

Susan gave an abbreviated account. Wheatley decided to let her. There would be plenty of time for further questioning over the next week or so. She told how the plan had been for 'Stephanie' to lie low while her 'disappearance' was reported. Then for Sir Tobias to also disappear and to book into a hotel under his 'real' name of Charles de Vere, saying that his wife would join him later.

"So, when I appeared at the Royal Albion Hotel that Friday, as far as they were concerned, I was Mrs de Vere," said Susan. "He was a bit surprised though! I told him Stephanie had sent me to tell him she was delayed but not to worry."

Susan continued, saying how 'Sir Tobias' or 'Charles de Vere' was displeased, both by her knowledge of their plans and by Stephanie's lateness.

"He was still in his dressing gown, lazy bugger," she said. "Probably expecting a bit of 'how's your father' as well, which he wasn't getting from me. Anyway, he turned away in disgust and that gave me my opportunity."

"Why?" asked Wheatley. "Why did you decide to…"

"Murder the bugger?" supplied Susan.

"Yes," said Wheatley. "And how? How did you expect to overpower a man so much bigger and more powerful than you?"

"I suppose I thought 'in for a penny…' I'd already done it once. Probably. At least she was dead and even if I couldn't remember it all, it seemed like I'd killed her. And if she deserved to die, he deserved it twice over. Three times."

Susan sighed then and looked down at her hands. While she was talking, she had been rubbing them together as if constantly washing them. A nervous habit, done subconsciously, Wheatley assumed, but now she seemed to become aware of it and shifted to place her hands under her thighs.

"I'd thought about it from time to time while I was playing at being a maid. Fantasized about it, I suppose, but never had the courage. After her, though, I decided I had to go through with it. That it was the right thing to do. For Millie. For Faith. For my self-respect. I never told you I was a nurse before I became a shop girl, did I?"

Wheatley was not thrown by the sudden change in direction of the conversation, remembering Mrs Stephens telling him that Susan had worked as a nurse before, as she put it, she decided that 'if she had wanted to spend her life skivvying, she'd have followed Millie into service.' But he suddenly realised that the remark carried more significance than he had given it. Another clue he had missed! While he was still castigating himself, Susan, sitting on her hands and leaning forward, carried on.

"Lots of poor beggars in hospital have blood poisoning and the only way to stop them dying is to lop off the infected bit. Fingers, hands, arms, legs all come off. To stop the bleeding while the surgeon cuts and saws and stitches, we'd put a loop of rope around the affected part, then insert a strong stick under the rope and twist. It's called a tourniquet and it's easy to tighten as much as you want. So that's what I used on him."

"And you," she said after a pause.

There were many thoughts that went through Wheatley's head at that point. That he hoped she hadn't meant to hurt him. That she just panicked when she thought, wrongly, that he knew she was the killer. That it was a spur of the moment thing. That if it was indeed 'spur of the moment,' where did she get the makings of a tourniquet from that evening? That possibly it was better not to know everything. What he said was, "You must have thought carefully about it."

Susan said 'Yes, of course', that it had taken all her effort to render unconscious a woman of her own size but once she remembered about tourniquets, she realised how she could overpower someone larger than her, even a heavy man.

"Or a skinny one," she said, swivelling to look at the detective, then hastily turning away again. "Anyway, I made a loop from a corset string. I know they're strong. They have to be to fasten a garment that squeezes your organs about so you can have a tiny waist, but I decided to double it just in case. Instead of the stick I used one of those peacock feather hat pins. Really strong they are, and I could wear them to fix my hat in place and no one would suspect their true purpose."

Up to this point Wheatley realised, he had been hoping that he could somehow excuse Susan. Perhaps suggest a lesser charge. That she didn't know what she was doing. After all, she said she didn't remember stabbing Miss Stephanie, only pulling the ties of the cape. Surely that was manslaughter at most? Perhaps a jury might be swayed by Millicent Stephens' tragic story. That Susan might only have to spend a short time in prison. Possibly in a hospital for the criminally insane at worst. But his hopes plummeted here. This admission sounded like premeditation. Sounded like murder.

"You say you don't remember the business with the hatpin? After the... er... choking, I mean."

And then more doubts assailed him. He was a policeman. A detective. Meant to be rational. Objective. Meant to enforce the law without fear or favour. And yet he seemed to be letting his personal feelings interfere with his duty.

"Not with her, no. It was all a blank." Susan stood up and began pacing the cell, frantically scrubbing at her hands again. "But with him. If anyone deserved to be attacked 'down there,' it was him."

And there it was, an admission of premeditated murder. Wheatley, the policeman, should have felt elation, but instead he felt sick. Susan was going to spend much of the rest of her life in gaol, even with the extenuating circumstances. And so he sat in silence while she returned to sit beside him on the bed and finished her story. There wasn't much more. She said what an effort it had been to pull the body onto the bed. That she had removed her dress before, in her words, 'starting on him' to avoid blood stains, 'though me shift were a right mess.' That she had told the hotel receptionist she was going shopping and 'not to disturb my husband.'

"I do regret misleading you," she said finally. "And - you know." Here she gently touched Wheatley's neck. "But I was frightened, thought I wanted to get away with it."

"But you don't now?"

"No. This seems right somehow. The story's been told and justice has been done. Now Millie, and Faith, *and* Dad can rest in peace. And so can I soon."

And how about your mother? Your friends? Me? thought Wheatley, but he kept his own counsel and Susan seemed to have run out of words so they sat in silence as the scant daylight through the barred windows high up close to the ceiling faded. Then Wheatley stood, said that he would see her again the next day, and exited the cell.

"Haven't you forgotten something, detective?" said Susan.

Wheatley thought for a moment, then said, "Goodnight, Susan, sleep tight," and carried on through the archway towards the stairs up to the Police Station above.

"Sweet thought, but that's not what I meant," said Susan.

This caused Wheatley to turn back. He was perplexed. What was he supposed to say?

"The cell door?" said Susan. "Shouldn't you lock it?"

Monday 5th March 1894

Wheatley had returned home feeling exhausted and took to his bed immediately after supper. He ignored the knock on the window of his wake-up call that morning but still felt lethargic despite a full night's sleep and a lie-in, it being almost eight am before he stirred. Rather than recovery, it was a sense of needing to do his duty, no matter how unpalatable, that drove him to ready himself for the day ahead. By ten of the clock, he was leaving his lodging house to go to work despite his shift not beginning until two in the afternoon.

The walk into Brighton along the seafront cleared the muddled feeling from his head and it was with a fresh intention to continue questioning Millie that he entered the Town Hall Police Station. Questioning *Susan,* he corrected himself. *The interrogation of Miss Susan Stephens, murderess.* Lost in thoughts of the direction his questioning should take, he was surprised to hear "Morning" as he crossed the parading hall and turned to witness the unprecedented occurrence of a nod and a greeting from Sergeant Johnson at the reception desk. There might even have been a smile on the sergeant's face, though it was difficult to tell with the unkemptness of his beard and moustaches. Bemused, Wheatley found this feeling of bonhomie to have also assaulted the Detective Office where Detective Edwards stood as Wheatley entered, vacating the desk chair.

"You're early, Wheatley," he said. "Not surprised, though. Come to glory in the praise, eh? You deserve it. Apprehension of a criminal at large and a full confession. The Inspector is cock-a-hoop."

The idea that he was expected to bask in approbation alarmed Wheatley and he rapidly demurred. "Not at all," he said. "Hardly a full confession either. I still have to get more evidence, especially of extenuating circumstances. Then we'll see if it will stand up in court."

"No need," said Edwards. "All done and dusted."

"What do you mean?" asked a confused Wheatley.

Detective Edwards reported that a magistrate's court had been convened by the Chief Constable that very morning. It had lasted almost no time at all.

"She pleaded guilty on all counts, so was arraigned to the County Assizes. She's in the cells now waiting for transfer to Lewes Prison."

"But she can't be. They can't have. What about the evidence? My evidence?"

"All unnecessary if she pleads guilty. And she maintains she don't want no brief neither, not that she could afford one, I suppose. Open and shut case. Just waiting for the judge to put his black hat on." Edwards resumed his seat as Wheatley headed for the door. "Where are you going?" Edwards called after his colleague, but the door had slammed shut before he received a reply.

Wheatley entered the holding area at a run, slamming into the cell door and slapping it in frustration when it failed to open.

"Door's locked, detective."

Susan was sitting demurely on the bed, fully dressed including coat and hat, her hands folded into her lap.

"What do you mean by pleading guilty? And offering no explanation, no reasons, no…"

"Calm down, detective. They asked me if I did it. I told them I did. That's all there is to it."

"That's *not* all there is to it," screamed Wheatley, gripping the cell-door bars. "How about your sister? What happened to her? That's extenuating circumstances. The jury will need to know that."

"No one needs to know nothing about my business," said Susan. "I know that justice has been done and that's enough for me."

Wheatley maintained his grip on the bars, but his head dropped, his agitation turned to despair. "You don't understand. With no explanation, no reason, you could hang. Millie, they could hang you."

"Justice has to be done, detective. An eye for an eye, remember?" Susan stood and took a strange pose, hands on hips, one leg thrust forwards, leaning back, a small smile on her lips. "Of course, I could always plead me belly."

For a moment this remark didn't register. Then Wheatley's head jerked up and he tried to take a step forward. This resulted in him ending up jammed against the cell door, his arms stretching towards her through the bars.

"Millie, you're not… Are you… Am I…?"

Susan almost grinned, but then the sadness returned to her eyes.

"Relax, detective, you're intact. As am I. I'm not with child. Couldn't be."

"But that evening. We… Didn't we?"

"What do you remember about that night, Wheatley?"

"I remember drinking brandy with you. I remember going upstairs meaning to search Miss Stephanie's room again." Here, Wheatley paused. He had raided his memory for any further recollections so many times since February the fourteenth, but as now, he could get no further. "I remember next morning. You in that nightgown…" He trailed off.

"Smoke and mirrors, detective. Smoke and mirrors."

"But Millie," began Wheatley. He didn't finish.

"Knock-out drops," said Susan. "Chloral hydrate. Another benefit of my nursing years. Needs to be dissolved in alcohol. Any non-harmful alcohol will do. Even 'Cognac from a single vineyard on the Charente'. All you did was snore. Loudly." Susan had taken up a stance with her arms folded, looking directly at Wheatley. "And my name is Susan. The Millie you remember don't exist. Never did. My Millie wasn't like that. Your Millie was just stringing you along, trying to mislead you. But now it's come to this, I'm actually glad you didn't fall for it. Not all of it, anyway."

"You called me Wheatley," said Wheatley.

"What?"

"Just now. You said, 'What do you remember Wheatley?' Not 'Detective'; 'Wheatley'."

This time Susan really smiled, then stepped forward and placed her hand between the bars to caress his cheek.

"That was Susan as said that," she said.

Their stillness together didn't last long.

"Sorry to interrupt, Detective Wheatley."

Wheatley and Susan each took a step backwards. Each dropped their hands to their sides as PC Jupp entered, accompanied by two gentlemen in uniform, HMP in brass letters adorning their kepis and stand-up jacket collars.

"Time to go, miss," said Jupp, turning a key in the cell door. "These two gents here has come to escort you."

*

"The young woman has made it very clear that she will not be making excuses for her crimes. Nor does she want any plea for clemency entered on her behalf and I respect her for that, lowly criminal that she is."

Inspector Cronin was at his pontificating best and determined to put a young detective in his place, thought Wheatley. Any respect for the inspector's handling of the Freemasonry side of things and the introduction to Colonel Gray disappeared into a simmering feeling of anger allied with abject helplessness.

"She has also made it clear that she will be pleading guilty on all accounts and so the Constabulary will not need to present any evidence. Which is good. Avoids any scandal you see. Any unsavoury reporting."

Any whiff of your rich friends being duped by a confidence trickster and his doxie, you mean, thought Wheatley. And of course, nothing about girls made pregnant or dying from illegal abortions. They didn't count. Didn't matter. Wheatley was trying to control his feelings, digging his fingernails into his palms before speaking. He tried a "But sir…"

"But nothing, Detective. I shall, of course, be present at the trial and if any additional evidence is requested by his honour the judge, I shall provide it. You, in the meantime, will resume your duties."

"Sir, I really think I need to investigate this further. And I certainly should be at the trial."

"You certainly should not! I thought I had made myself clear, Detective Constable, but just to repeat: you will have no further contact with the accused, and you will not attend the trial." The steel that Wheatley had witnessed in Cronin on his last visit to the Inspector's office asserted itself again here. "And just in case you feel inclined to disobey these orders, know that I have spoken with the Warden of Her Majesty's Prison, Lewes, and with the Chief Constable of East Sussex and we have agreed that you will be refused entry both to the prison and the courtroom until further notice."

Wheatley was distraught. It all seemed hopeless and he realised his efforts to intercede on Susan's behalf seemed doomed to failure.

"Will that be all, sir?" was all he said, though he seethed inside.

The Inspector had been standing behind his desk with Wheatley on the other side, facing him. Now he sighed and sank into his chair.

"Your work on this case was exemplary, Wheatley. Dash me, I don't know how you solved it. A woman committing murder. Twice! Who'd have believed it?"

If Wheatley had been feeling more charitable towards Inspector Cronin, he might have admitted that he, also, was at a loss to explain his success and that it had taken an attempt on his life for the penny to drop. But he wasn't, so he didn't. Instead, he maintained a stony silence.

"You are a good detective," continued the Inspector, "though not necessarily a good policeman. You get too involved in your cases. In an emotional sense. We need to remain aloof, Wheatley. See the bigger picture, eh? Maintain a dignified demeanour."

This was also met with silence, Wheatley staring over the Inspector's shoulder.

"Very well, that's all. You may resume your duties."

"Sir, my duty is to see this case through. There are so many circumstances to be reviewed."

"Your *other* duties, I meant. I believe I have made myself clear in reference to the murder case."

"Sir, I must protest..." began Wheatley, but to no avail.

"Protest noted. That will be all."

"Sir..."

"Dismissed, Detective Constable! Let this be the end to it."

Inspector Cronin swivelled his chair to gaze out of the window. Wheatley paused for a moment, realised there was nothing he could do, turned on his heel and strode from the room. As he reached the office door, he noticed that the silver-topped Malacca cane that Colonel Gray had borrowed and presumably returned was back in the inspector's umbrella stand. Seizing the stick without asking permission, Wheatley exited the office, deliberately not closing the door behind him.

Wednesday 14th March 1894

On the day of the trial Wheatley was on the corner of Jew Street and Church Street in Brighton, at the premises of Jakub Zimmerman, Pawnbroker, waiting to be let into the shop, holding a lady's ostrich feather hat.

"I shan't be long, Mr Jupp," said Wheatley as a buzz from the shop door indicated he could enter. PC Jupp nodded his head, then stared at his boots. He had been subdued since being placed on 'watch duty' by the Inspector of Detectives over a week ago. Watch duty consisted of accompanying Detective Wheatley wherever he went and reporting back to Inspector Cronin as to the detective's movements. Wheatley assumed Jupp's subdued demeanour was because he resented, and hopefully, disapproved of his assignment, but that the constable was far too professional to say so. Instead he had restricted his comments to practicalities, any further conversation being almost completely absent. In some ways Wheatley was grateful to be shadowed. It removed the responsibility he felt to appear at the trial on behalf of Susan Stephens. After all, how could he get to the Courthouse when his every movement was scrutinised? His vision of giving testimony which would sway the jury to leniency was a pipedream, he knew. It was clear that

Susan had made up her mind not to make any statement but 'guilty,' and showed typical female obstinacy by maintaining this. He had tried writing to her, but all letters had been returned unopened. He removed his pocket watch from his waistcoat to check the time.

"A penny for them, Mr Policeman."

The detective jerked back to attentiveness to see the pawnshop proprietor peering through the bars which surrounded the counter, blocking the rear of the shop from customers in the main area.

"Must be five minutes you been standing there gazing at that watch."

"I'm sorry, Mr Zimmerman, lost in thought. I've come to return this," said Wheatley, placing his watch back in his pocket with one hand while holding aloft the hat in the other.

"Yahweh be praised, an honest policeman," said Zimmerman. Reaching below the counter, he said, "I'll get your account."

"I don't think that will be necessary," said Wheatley, determined not to be taken advantage of this time. Zimmerman paused in his movements and looked at the detective. Then Wheatley noticed his eyes flick to the window where PC Jupp was peering into the shop. There was a pause before the shopkeeper withdrew his hand and sat up slowly.

"Of course, forgive me. No charge. Now what do we have here?"

Wheatley laid the hat on the counter. Jakub Zimmerman carefully drew it through the screen and in a familiar movement, blew gently on the ostrich feather and stroked it carefully.

"Such a beautiful plume," said Zimmerman. "I wonder what happened to the lady who pledged it. The one with the lovely eyes."

"At this moment, she's answering charges at the Spring Assizes in Lewes."

"Really?" Jakub's eyebrows were raised.

"Murder," said Wheatley, speaking before he thought.

The old man seemed to be waiting for more. "Did she do it?" he said when no further information was forthcoming.

"Yes, I'm afraid she did," said Wheatley.

"Who would believe it? That beautiful girl? Such a waste," said Zimmerman.

"Yes, such a waste," said Wheatley as he turned on his heel to leave the shop, speaking so quietly that he could hardly be heard.

Thursday 12th April 1894

Wheatley was surprised by the number of passengers on the Lewes train that early in the morning. He had spent the journey from Brighton sharing a compartment with a group of Quakers, judging by their sombre dress and use of the antiquated 'thee' and 'thou' by which they occasionally addressed each other. *Society of Friends*, he mentally corrected himself. As the train pulled into Lewes station, he could see a similar group waiting on the platform, and upon disembarking watched them join forces and move as one uphill towards the castle. Wheatley followed, turning left along the High Street once the climb to the castle was over. As he got closer to the prison, he was joined by a trickle of pedestrians headed in the same direction. He arrived at the prison gates at exactly ten minutes to eight; by then a fair crowd had gathered. He noticed Mrs Stephens accompanied by George Small, Fanny Bunting, the barman from the Friar's Oak and a parson he did not recognise. The barman had his arm around Fanny's shoulders while George, Mrs Stephens and the parson stood in silence. Wheatley acknowledged them by raising his hat. Only the parson replied to his greeting with a dignified dip of his head. The others stared stonily at him and Wheatley decided to take station under a tree away from the group.

The gathering outside of the prison was subdued and orderly but still two uniformed constables policed the crowd. They were standing close to Wheatley who nodded a greeting. They too replied with a stony stare. Wheatley experienced a pang of embarrassment, embarrassment that came too frequently for him, he thought. *Obviously they don't acknowledge me as a fellow officer. After all, I'm in plainclothes and from a different constabulary*, he admonished himself. Not wishing to draw attention to himself further, Wheatley quietly studied the small crowd gathered outside of the prison gates. Apart from the Hassocks contingent and one or two obvious thrill-seekers, there were also several religious groups gathered about their various pastors. The Quakers stood in a circle facing inwards in silence. Looking beyond them, Wheatley was surprised to see Shadrach Mears, standing alone and wearing a top hat and a somewhat short threadbare overcoat, his brown overall showing below it. Wheatley decided to risk one more acknowledgement and this time it was reciprocated, Shadrach solemnly raising his hat. Having replaced it, he bent and picked up a placard which had been on the ground next to his feet. Written on it was 'Leviticus 24:19–21' and beneath that 'John 8:7'. Wheatley was considering going over to him and asking about the verses when the first chime of eight am sounded from the prison clock. There was a gasp from the crowd followed by a profound stillness through the next seven chimes. Then, a complete silence. Even the birds seemed to have ceased singing and Wheatley noticed that the traffic on the High Street had stopped. The drovers, carters and pedestrians all paused, the men removing their hats. The silence was broken by whispered prayers and subdued sobbing from the Widow Stephens and Fanny Bunting. In a heartbeat all became normal again, the traffic moving, the thrill-seekers making their way home, leaving a small crowd gathered around the prison gate.

After what seemed to Wheatley a considerable time but was probably a matter of minutes, a postern in the prison door opened and a uniformed warder stepped through to pin a notice on the main gates. The first people to move towards it once the warder had returned inside were the Hassocks contingent, Mrs Stephens to the fore. She stood for a few seconds, her lips moving as she read. Then a fearful moan came from her, developing into a screamed *"No,"* and she would have collapsed to the floor had George Small's sturdy frame not been there to support her. In the shocked silence following her scream, Wheatley heard a voice he recognised.

Abide with me, fast falls the eventide
The darkness deepens, Lord, with me abide.

Shadrach Mears' high tenor voice rang out.

When other helpers fall and comforts flee,
Help of the Helpless. Oh, abide with me.

Raggedly, the remains of the crowd joined in

Swift to its close ebbs out life's little day
Earth's joys grow dim, its glories pass away
Change and decay in all around I see
O Thou who changest not, abide with me.

Shadrach had been moving slowly while he sang and as he reached his crescendo, he placed his placard under his arm and set off along the High Street in the direction of Juggs Lane, a droveway between Lewes and Brighton. A long walk for the portly mortuary attendant, thought Wheatley. Slowly the spectators filed past the notice on the doorway. Mrs Stephens, Fanny and George Small had waited where they stood and were the last of the crowd to leave, followed by the two policemen. Wheatley was left alone beneath the tree. He waited for a while, then made his way to the main gate. He had never seen a notice of execution before. It was brief and pitiless, detailing only the name of the person executed, the signature of the doctor who certified death and countersigned by the East Sussex Coroner on behalf of the jury who had witnessed the hanging. And there it was in stark black and white.

Death by lawful execution, Susan Agnes Stephens on this twelfth day of April in the year of Our Lord, eighteen hundred and ninety-four.

Wheatley felt as though his chest was full. As if difficulty in breathing would be his normal way of being from now on. As if the heaviness of his limbs would last forever. Slowly he made his way along the High Street, considering the thoughtfulness of the various religious groups who had set vigil for Susan's last moments, of the anguish of a mother losing her final daughter and the friends who supported her, of the kindness of Shadrach Mears.

In this frame of mind, he entered the church of St Michael in Lewes, thankfully empty at that time of day. He sat for a while, wondering whether it would be wrong in so many ways to pray for the soul of Susan Stephens, one of his religions damning her for eternity for her actions while the other denied the existence of an afterlife altogether. He settled for thinking fondly of her. Then he stood and moved to the lectern and opened the King James Bible to the passages Shadrach had displayed on his hand-made poster. Here he found no definitive answer, just the contradictions and uncertainty that seemed to haunt him no matter how hard he tried to find absolute truth.

*

Leviticus 24:19–21

And if a man cause a blemish in his neighbour; as he hath done, so shall it be done to him; Breach for breach, eye for eye, tooth for tooth; as he has caused a blemish in a man, so shall it be done to him again. And he that killeth a beast, he shall restore it: and he that killeth a man, he shall be put to death.

St. John 8:7

So when they continued asking him, he lifted up himself, and said unto them: He that is without sin among you, let him first cast a stone at her.

The End

But never fear, Wheatley will return.

Barry Silsby is a writer and educator and that rarest of beasts — a native Brightonian still living by the sea in the city of Brighton and Hove (www.barrysilsby.org).

Photograph by Sarah Ketelaars
(www.sarahketelaars.com)

Acknowledgements

To all my writing group friends, past and present. You know who you are.

To the 'Bookends' writers and quizzers: Ally, Chris, Meriel, Sally and Thelma. We've come a long way together.

To our writing guru extraordinaire Susannah Waters (www.susannahwaters.com).

To Dr Liz Archer, who put me right on all matters medical and suffered my inaccuracies. Any mistakes are mine, not hers.

Thank you all for your support and friendship.